W9-BYL-866

ORDINARY MIRACLES

ORDINARY MIRACLES

STEPHANIE S. TOLAN

MORROW JUNIOR BOOKS
NEW YORK

Special thanks are due to three people who helped me with the scientific aspects of this book: Dr. Timothy Perper, whose dual persona of scientist and storyteller provided vital support during the writing process; Dr. Craig Taylor, of the Woods Hole Oceanographic Institute, who helped me figure out what could and could not be; and "our kid, the doctor," Robert W. Tolan, Jr., M.D., whose medical expertise was essential and whose critical eye is always valued.

Published by Morrow Junior Books
a division of William Morrow and Company, Inc.
1350 Avenue of the Americas, New York, NY 10019
www.williammorrow.com

Printed in the United States of America.

1 3 5 7 9 10 8 6 4 2

Library of Congress Cataloging-in-Publication Data
Tolan, Stephanie S.
Ordinary miracles / Stephanie S. Tolan.
p. cm.
Summary: Tired of being a twin, Mark tries to spend more time away from his twin brother and meets a scientist who challenges some of Mark's long-held Christian beliefs about heaven, God, prayer, and death.
ISBN 0-688-16269-X
[1. Twins—Fiction. 2. Brothers—Fiction. 3. Christian life—Fiction.]
I. Title. PZ7.T57350r 1999 [Fic]—dc21 99-13658 CIP

With gratitude for—and to—the Great Mystery

Science without religion is lame;
religion without science is blind.
—Albert Einstein

CHAPTER ONE

To see how they look, most people have to have a mirror. And even if they stare into that mirror very hard, all they can see about themselves is one side with eyes that don't move. Have you ever tried to see your eyes move in a mirror? You can't. Not even a little! The best you can do is move your head around them so that the pupil and iris parts are in a different place in your eye space. Up or down or left or right. But that isn't the same as seeing your eyes move. Try it if you never have. It's very weird. You can't watch yourself roll your eyes, or close them, either.

And you can't see yourself from the back—unless you use two mirrors. I guess if your family has enough money for a video camera (my family doesn't), you can watch videos of yourself, but even though videotape can show you moving, it's still flat. Two-dimensional. Not really real. So you don't really know how you look. Not to other people.

I do, though. I can watch myself from the front and the back, sideways, above and below. In 3-D. I can watch my eyes move. I can see how I look with my eyes closed. I can even watch myself sleeping. Because everywhere I go in my life, there's my identical twin. When I say identical, I *mean* identical. Neither one of us has what the police would call a distinguishing feature. Just going by looks, my twin might as well *be* me. In other ways, too. He loves to play soccer. I love to play soccer. His favorite color is blue; my favorite color is blue. We laugh at the same jokes. The same things make us sad. And sometimes we even have the same dreams. The first time we knew that was when we both woke up screaming at the same time one night when we were about four. The same hairy monster with the same glowing red eyes had been chasing us both. Not even Mom and Dad know that about us, though.

Being almost exactly the same doesn't mean we never argue. But even arguing's weird, because it's like arguing with yourself—except he's better at it. See, that's how we both know we really aren't the same person. He's smarter. And faster. And stronger. Not a lot, just enough.

His name is Matthew David Filkins. That's because he was born first—a whole minute and ten seconds before I was. (When I used to say that wasn't enough older to mean anything, he would make me count up to seventy—"one Mississippi, two Mississippi, three Mississippi"—just to prove how very long it was.) If I'd come out first, *I'd* have been named Matthew. But thanks to those seventy seconds, I'm Mark. Mark Thomas Filkins. Matthew and Mark, get it? Like the Gospels. That's how it always goes. Matthew and Mark. Nobody ever says Mark and Matthew. I've wondered a lot whether it would have made a difference. Whether if I'd come out first I'd actually have *been* Matthew. And he'd have been me.

We have a younger brother named—guess what? Luke. He was born a year and forty-eight days after we were. One time, Matthew held him down and tried to make him count to 35,683,200, which is how many seconds there are between our birthday and his, but Luke isn't easy to hang on to. Before he even got to ten, he'd wiggled himself loose and kicked Matthew hard enough in the shin to leave a bruise. It was just as well. Matthew hadn't thought about the fact that counting all those seconds would take the whole year and forty-eight days!

Our dad's a minister. So was his dad and his dad before him and his dad before him. Mom and Dad were planning to raise four boys who would grow up to be ministers, just like the boys of the four generations of Filkinses before us. But things don't always work out the way you planned, not even for ministers of God.

Two years later, they had a girl. They didn't want to try again, in case they got another girl, so they just named the baby Johnna and gave up on the plan.

In some denominations, a girl could grow up to be a minister, but even though Dad has his own church—the Rock of Ages Community Church—we're sort of connected to a whole bunch of others, and so far there aren't any women ministers in any of them. Dad says there never will be. Johnna's in fifth grade now, and at least as stubborn and ornery as Luke. Even if she had been a boy, I don't think Mom and Dad could have counted on her to be what they wanted her to be.

Matthew and I are in the eighth grade at John Glenn Junior High School in Bradyville, Ohio. That means we're not the oldest kids in the school. There are ninth graders above us, which drives Matthew crazy. He can't wait till next year.

Not that either of us will probably get much out of being big-shot ninth graders. We aren't exactly popular. It's hard to fit in when you aren't allowed to go to movies or watch the shows everybody else watches on television and you don't have a computer or Nintendo and you can't afford to plunk down a hundred bucks for a pair of basketball shoes. Being twins gets us a lot of attention, though. Nobody can tell us apart. That used to mess up the teachers and everybody else, so I got an identification bracelet with my name on it. I wear it all the time, and since Matthew doesn't have one, all anybody has to do to know which is which is to look at our left wrists. If there's a bracelet, it's Mark. If there's not, it's Matthew. We could play practical jokes on everybody if we switched, but we hardly ever do. That's because Matthew doesn't really want to be mistaken for me.

I can see what I look like when I look at Matthew, but when he looks at me, all he sees is his shadow.

Mom says that brothers should never compete and never compare—even regular brothers, much less twins. Comparisons make room for all sorts of bad things—like vanity and envy. And brothers are supposed to love each other. "Love suffers long and is kind; love envies not. Love vaunts not itself, is not puffed up." That's from First Corinthians. Matthew and I love each other. We do. We're twins. We come from the same egg and the same sperm that got together to make one person and then split into two people instead. How could we not love each other? Except that when I hear "Love suffers long," I think of me, and when I hear "Love is not puffed up," I want to remind Matthew about that. I don't. I don't. I never, ever do. "Love is kind."

But the September Saturday afternoon Dad told us we were old enough to begin really helping out at church services (we've been ushers and passed the collection plate ever since we were old enough to hold it), I wasn't *feeling* so kind. Dad had called us into the dining room, where he'd been working on his Sunday sermon.

"I think the two of you are old enough now to handle a major church responsibility," he said, and I could tell by the "Reverend Filkins" voice he was using that he wanted us to understand that what he was about to say was really important. "I'd like the two of you to write—and deliver—the sermon for next Wednesday's prayer meeting. The verse I'm using for tomorrow is 'For thou has been a strength to the poor, a strength to the needy in his distress.' I'd like you to come up with something that relates to it."

Matthew looked at me and I looked at him. Both of us were seeing the same expression. Surprise. The most Dad had ever let us do before was read the day's Bible verses on Sunday. Writing a sermon, even as short as the one for Wednesday prayer meeting, was something else again. The other thing we saw was fear. At least I saw fear in Matthew's eyes. What he was seeing in mine had to be more like terror. Stark, cold, heart-stopping, mind-numbing terror. Who would want to listen to a sermon preached by kids? Not that there were ever many people at the Wednesday night service to listen. Still—even old Mrs. Quigley, who never missed, came to hear Dad preach, not us.

The fear went out of Matthew's eyes in a hurry, though, and they glazed over the way they do when he's thinking very hard. I could practically hear his brain clicking away.

I looked back at Dad and noticed behind his smile that look he always gets when he's getting ready for Sunday service. Preaching is not what Dad likes best about being a minister. What he likes is finding people who need help and helping them. Getting them food or clothes or someplace to stay or a job or something. He likes helping people get through the red tape and hassles at the county welfare office or Health and Human Services. He even likes visiting old people, and people in the hospital. He shares the Gospel as well as anybody, but he likes to do it one-on-one. He's more about action than he is about words.

The dining room table was covered with crumpled-up pieces of yellow paper from his legal pad. And there were only a couple of lines of writing on the pad itself. It was after five o'clock. Usually by this time on a Saturday, the sermon is all done and Mom has already typed it out on the old Selectric in the church office so Dad can practice it after dinner.

He saw me looking at the crumpled-up paper. "To tell you the truth, boys, the idea of doing two sermons this week is more than I can handle right now. I spent the morning and most of the afternoon helping Elbert Hode haul grass clippings. He's been using that old truck for his lawn service. You know, the one I got the Wendell Brothers Garage to donate to the church. But the stupid thing broke down on the way to the county compost heap this morning. We had to put all the clippings in bags and then take the bags in the Buick. Even using the trunk and the backseat both, it took eleven trips, and I'm too bushed to get tomorrow's sermon done, let alone think about a tie-in for Wednesday night."

No wonder he thought of that verse for the sermon, I thought. "For thou has been a strength to the poor. . . ." Only it wasn't *God* who'd spent the whole of Saturday helping Elbert Hode; it was Dad. I didn't say anything. He would just say he was God's instrument. Matthew was still glazed. By now he probably had a whole sermon sketched out in his mind.

Dad sighed and rubbed at his bald spot. Mom says he'll be a billiard ball in no time if he doesn't stop rubbing his hair off. I don't think he even knows he's doing it. "There isn't enough in the verse I chose for a Wednesday sermon, too." Dad waved at the crumpled papers on the table and rubbed his bald spot again. "There's not really enough there for tomorrow!"

"That's okay," Matthew said. "We can come up with something." I could tell by the tone of his voice that he already had.

"How can two people give one sermon?" I asked.

Dad grinned. "Make it a two-parter. Or a dialogue maybe."

Matthew nodded. We left Dad to his job then. I watched my back heading upstairs toward the bedroom we share with Luke. Matthew didn't even glance over his shoulder at his shadow following him up.

CHAPTER TWO

About halfway up the stairs, a Bible verse occurred to me that would connect really well with the verse Dad had chosen. It wasn't just one verse—it was really five: Matthew 7:7–11. I figured that was okay because it would take longer to read the text, so we wouldn't have to think up as much to say about it. The first part of it was "Ask, and it shall be given you; seek, and ye shall find; knock, and it shall be opened unto you." There's pretty much the same thing in Luke 11, but this one's the version that's most well known. I didn't say anything, though. I knew perfectly well we'd end up using the one Matthew had thought of, not mine. That's just the way it works between us.

When we got up to the bedroom we share with Luke, Matthew sat down at the desk. Our room has one bunk bed and one twin bed, a big dresser Matthew and I share, a little one for Luke, and one desk with one chair. All of this furniture came from church rummage sales or secondhand stores, except for the desk, which Dad got for free when the Third National Bank burned. It's a metal desk, gray except for the left side, which is black and sort of melted, so the whole desktop slopes down to the left a little bit. Luke mostly does his homework downstairs on the dining room table, but Matthew likes to work at the desk. So mostly he does. I like to work there, too, but I don't very often because we're usually doing our homework at the same time. Somehow the desk just seems to *belong* to Matthew.

I fluffed up Luke's pillow and sat on his bed. "So?" I asked.

"Matthew seven: seven through eleven," Matthew said. "'Ask and it shall—'"

"'Be given you,'" I said. We finished it together. "'Seek, and ye shall find.'" You might be shaking your head right now about the coincidence. Out of the whole huge Bible (and Matthew and I know a whole lot of it by heart), we both came up with exactly the same verses. But it wasn't a coincidence! It was what we call "the twin thing." It happens all the time.

Except that this time it made me mad. If that was the verse he'd thought up right away down in the dining room, it meant he'd thought of it first. So had *I* really thought of it? Or had I just picked it up from his mind after he'd thought of it?

"So? What do you think?" Matthew asked. He didn't know that I'd thought of the same text. He wasn't surprised that I could say it with him, of course. There aren't a lot of Bible texts that one of us could start that the other couldn't finish. For almost as long as either of us can remember, Dad has played a game with us at dinner, where he quotes a Bible verse and we have to say what it is. At least that's how he used to play it when we were little. Now the whole family plays. We take turns being "it" and giving the verse for someone else to identify. Johnna and Luke aren't very good at it, but Matthew and I always have been.

Probably that's because we learned to read from a children's Bible our grandpa Filkins sent us from Texas for our fourth birthday. And we went right on reading the Bible when we outgrew that one—and competing to see who could win the game more often. We're mostly pretty even, and sometimes I wonder if that isn't because of the twin thing, too.

"So?" Matthew said again. "What do you think?"

I didn't answer right away. I just sat there, rubbing my hand across the ridges on Luke's bedspread. I felt like there was a snake in the middle of me, wiggling around, biting at me, sinking its sharp little fangs into my gut. I looked over at Matthew, who was leaning back in the chair, waiting for me to answer. And all of a sudden, I didn't want to be a twin anymore. I didn't want to see my face and my body across the room from me. Unless, like anybody else, I was looking in a mirror. I didn't want to like the same things Matthew liked or dream the same dreams. And I certainly didn't want to think the same thoughts five minutes after he did. "I have a better one," I said, even though I didn't.

"But this one fits really well with Dad's," he said.

"And I suppose you've worked out what we're going to say. Both of us."

Matthew, his face as innocent as a two-year-old's, nodded. "Most of it." It hadn't even occurred to him that there might be anything I wouldn't like about his thinking up the whole thing, my part as well as his. That was one trouble with the way I was feeling right then. That Matthew wouldn't even be able to understand it. He wasn't trying to make me feel bad. It just didn't occur to him that I might. Just the way it didn't occur to him that he didn't have to wear an ID bracelet—as if he was the *real* kid and I was the copy that had to be identified as a copy. "We don't need another verse. Here's what I thought we should say. . . ."

While he talked, my mind must have been clicking, too. I was running through all the texts I could remember that had anything to do with God helping people. There were a lot, of course. Now I just grabbed at one and interrupted him. "Matthew six: twenty-eight through thirty-four."

Matthew's eyebrows went up. "'Consider the lilies'? That doesn't fit 'For thou has been a strength to the poor.'"

"Sure it does. 'Wherefore, if God so clothes the grass of the field, which today is alive and tomorrow is cast into the oven, shall he not much more clothe you, O ye of little faith? Therefore take no thought, saying, "What shall we eat?" or "What shall we drink?" or "Wherewithal shall we be clothed?" For your heavenly Father knoweth that ye have need of all these things.'" I was still thinking fast. "It's even better than 'Ask, and it shall be given you,' because this one says you don't even have to ask. God already knows what you need, so he'll be a strength to the poor, just like he is to the lilies in the field. All you have to have is faith!"

Matthew thought about it a minute, shaking his head a little. "Mine fits better," he said.

"Says you."

He shrugged. "Okay, then, we can do both. I'll write mine and you write yours. We can each have about five minutes."

With that, he swung around on the chair, pulled a spiral notebook out of the desk drawer, and started writing.

The snake was still biting me in the gut. Why did Matthew have to be so nice about it? Why couldn't he have put up a fight? His verse was fine. Great. It was the same one I'd wanted, really. I watched his back as he bent over the notebook on the desk, writing away. Right-handed, of course. Like me. Luke is left-handed. But then, he is different from us. He is *allowed* to be different.

Matthew was working as cheerfully as if nothing at all had just happened. What *had* happened? I didn't know. Except that I was sitting there with that snake chewing away in the middle of me.

When Luke called up to tell us to come down for supper, Matthew was just finishing his and I had moved over to my bed—the bottom bunk—and was sitting there with almost as many crumpled pieces of paper around me as there'd been around Dad in the dining room.

CHAPTER THREE

For three days after that stupid snake started gnawing on me, things went okay. Sort of normal. I finished writing what I wanted to say about my Bible text Sunday afternoon after church, and after supper Monday night Dad had us practice, with him giving pointers.

He liked the idea of us using different texts, and he agreed with me that "Consider the lilies" showed an even greater power of faith than "Ask, and it shall be given you." So he wanted Matthew to do his first and me to follow. That was fine with Matthew, but it scared me worse than going first would have. I figured whoever went first had the advantage of novelty. Everybody would be extra forgiving, since no kid had ever preached at our church before. But the second—by then they'd be over the shock and would be listening harder, expecting more. Second was worse every way I could think of. If Matthew was good, then I'd have to live up to what he did, and if he wasn't, everybody would already be grumpy by the time I got up to the pulpit. Besides, I worried how we'd look.

Physically, we take after Dad. He's not real tall. Sort of chunky. Squarish. Us, too. We get all sorts of attention for being identical twins, but it isn't because of how great we look. I didn't like the thought of standing up there at the pulpit with everybody having nothing to look at but us. At least we'd have on the navy blue choir robes we wear when we usher and pass the collection plate. They cover you up pretty good. I was sure the congregation would prefer to look at Luke. I've seen girls staring at him at school when he's just sitting around doing nothing.

Dad said we'd both done good work and we'd give an excellent accounting of ourselves. On the other hand, he pretty much had to say that. He was our father, after all, and having us preach was his idea in the first place.

Wednesday was not a great day. Matthew and I are both in the same classes at school (as we have been every year except second grade, which was the worst year of our lives), and all day I kept trying to decide whether he was really as calm as he looked. Usually I can tell how he feels just by looking at him. But not that day. I was too caught up in how I felt, I guess.

I'd had a dream just before I woke up that morning. Not a dream. A straight-out nightmare. I'd been standing at the pulpit in front of the whole congregation (not just a regular little Wednesday night congregation at the Rock of Ages Community Church, but the congregation from the Crystal Cathedral on TV, hundreds and hundreds of them) and I went completely blank. We're supposed to look out at the people as we talk—"Talk right *to* them," Dad said. But he had us write notes on three-by-five cards that we could look at if we got stuck, and in the dream I had the cards in my hand. But when I went to look at them, I'd gone blind. Completely blind. Everything was as dark as if somebody had pulled a black hood over my head. I blinked a couple of times and my eyesight came back. Then I almost wished it hadn't, because I could see all those people in the pews staring at me, starting to laugh. And I could see the cards in my hand, shaking like leaves in the wind. Only there wasn't any writing on them. So I just stood there, opening and closing my mouth like a fish out of water while the congregation laughed and pointed. Then Matthew came up and pushed me out of the way, and I looked down and saw that I had nothing on except my underwear. I was trying to hide behind the altar, and Matthew, his voice sounding exactly like Dad's, was preaching my part of the sermon when I woke up. I lay there a long time, listening to Matthew breathe. The snake was back, chewing away.

No matter what I tried to do all day, the dream was there, running itself over and over again. I couldn't even concentrate on math, my favorite subject. And I barely heard Mrs. Gerston's announcement in science class. Something about a guest teacher. But I was stuck in that nightmare, remembering those laughing faces and Matthew's voice preaching my sermon.

It turned out Matthew was nervous, too. He told me while we ate lunch. While *he* ate lunch. We'd made ourselves tuna sandwiches that morning, but now the smell of tuna made me sick to my stomach. Matthew hadn't had my dream, but he had his own worries. "What if we have to go to the bathroom right in the middle?"

I don't know why I hadn't thought of that one. Bad stress makes us have to pee. It can make life very tough sometimes. "Just hold it till we're done," I said. "It's only ten minutes." But I wasn't sure *I* could hold it for ten minutes. Not and also remember what I was supposed to say. Now I had a whole new thing to worry about. "We just have to pee right before, that's all. Like before an exam."

After school we had soccer practice. Zach Soames and Evan Elsasser met us in the hall, but Matthew told them to go on without us. When they were gone, he said we wouldn't be able to play soccer worth anything anyway, nervous as we were. "We need to practice the sermon some more," he said. "We can do it in the church and get Johnna to sit in the back pew to make sure we're talking loud enough."

I thought of the little pile of three-by-five cards

next to my bed at home, and how much better I'd feel if I had more practice. A whole lot more practice. But I kept thinking about how he said "we" without even asking me how I felt. When I opened my mouth, instead of agreeing with him, I said I was going to soccer. "It wouldn't be fair to Coach MacMahon if we both cut."

Matthew shrugged. "Okay. See you later. I'll be outta the shower before you come home."

I've hardly ever played soccer without Matthew before, and at first, when we started our scrimmage, I almost didn't know what to do, how to play. We play center forward and right wing, and I'm used to knowing he's there to my left. The coach is always trying to get team members to pass more, but he doesn't have to push that with us. We do a whole lot of passing back and forth and we hardly ever miss, because we can sort of read each other's playing. With me as center and Zach in as right wing, nothing seemed to work. He was never where I expected him to be. After practice Coach MacMahon clapped me on the back. "Your concentration and timing were off today," he said, as if I hadn't noticed. "I think I should split you and Matt up and move you around a little more. Maybe you're getting a little too dependent on each other."

I nodded. Yeah. Maybe.

I should have gone straight home then to get my shower and go over my notes. But our house isn't very big, and no matter where Matthew was practicing his part of the sermon, I'd be able to hear him. I knew that no matter how he was doing, it would sound better to me than me. "Turn it over," Mom tells us when something is really bugging us. She means that when you have faith in God, he "makes all things right." All you have to do is turn the problem over to him and he'll take care of it.

Okay, God, I thought. I'm passing this one off to you. If I'm supposed to make a goal tonight, it's gotta be your doing! Instead of heading for home, I went on past the school soccer field into Monument Park and down toward the lake. There's a paved trail around the lake that's usually full of people exercising, walking or jogging, pushing baby strollers or walking dogs or skating. I cut across the trail and down to a willow tree by the shore. It's an old tree with big old trailing branches that make a canopy all around the trunk. Matthew and I used to play there when we were little, pretending it was a cave or a tent or headquarters for our army when we were playing with other kids from the neighborhood. Now I just wanted to sit for a while someplace familiar and comfortable, where nobody would notice me, *not* thinking about having to preach in a couple of hours.

As usual, there were a bunch of geese and some mallard ducks on the lake, coasting around near the shore, hoping somebody would come along to feed them popcorn or bread crumbs. I pushed through the willow branches and into the dim, quiet space beneath. A cluster of gnats was there, too, and I waved them away as I sat down facing the water. For a while I watched the ducks through the willow leaves, wondering what it was they were finding to eat when they ducked their heads down under the water. All that was down there as far as I knew was slimy mud that squelched up between your toes and pulled at your bare feet. Swimming isn't allowed in the lake, but we'd gone wading there a lot when we were little. After a while the birds came up out of the water and settled down on the grass, some of them tucking their heads under their wings for a little nap.

I'd just decided that a couple of hours from now the congregation was probably going to look like that while I was preaching, when the ducks suddenly scattered, quacking and flapping in panic as they headed for the water, some running, some lifting off to fly farther out into the water. A white-and-brown dog with floppy ears came thundering down the bank, its stub of a tail circling frantically, plunged into the lake, and, when the water was up to its belly, stood barking as the ducks settled themselves well out beyond it. Can't swim, I thought. Lucky for the ducks.

I heard a low whistle and the dog stopped barking and glanced back over its shoulder. A man came into view then, his back to me as he walked down to the edge of the water. He was tall and broad-shouldered, dressed in baggy jeans and a loose-fitting plaid shirt, with a baseball cap on a thatch of shaggy grayish brown hair. He stood for a moment or two, and now the dog turned sideways, looking first toward him and then toward the ducks, as if it was afraid of missing something. Then the man leaned down and picked something up off the ground. Now the dog lost all interest in the ducks. Wiggling and whining, it bounced toward the man and then back, its front feet down, its head low and its rear end high. The man threw what he had picked up into the water, midway between the dog and the cluster of ducks. As soon as it left the man's hand, the dog was heading for where it was going to hit the water, just the way Matthew would head for where the soccer ball was going to be when I passed it. But when the splash came as the thing hit the water, nothing floated back to the surface. Whatever the man had thrown, it had gone straight down.

I felt sorry for the dog, which wouldn't be able to find what it was after when it got out there. But it kept on swimming, and when it came to where the splash had been, it suddenly ducked its head down and—just like one of the ducks—headed straight under the water, its rear end, with the still-circling stump of a tail, sticking straight up toward the sky. After a second, even its tail disappeared. I pushed myself to my feet and broke out of the cover of the willow branches. I think maybe I had some idea of jumping in to rescue the fool dog or something, but suddenly its nose broke the water a little way away from where it had gone down. It had something in its mouth as its whole head came up, and it began swimming back toward the shore, slowing after a moment to shake the water out of its ears. When it reached water shallow enough to get its feet on the bottom, it began trotting, tail still circling, and came out of the water, dripping all over, and set a rock on the ground at the man's feet.

It shook itself, spraying water on the man's jeans, then began its dance all over again, frisking and barking, begging to have the rock thrown, just as I'd watched dogs begging their masters to throw a stick or a ball for them to retrieve. The man threw the rock again, and again the dog swam to where it had disappeared and then dived for it. This time the rock had landed in water shallow enough that the dog's tail never disappeared below the surface of the water. It was back on land in no time, shaking water and barking to have the rock thrown again.

After a few more throws, the man went to sit on a bench by the water's edge and went on throwing the rock from there. I couldn't pull myself away from the sight of this diving dog. I'd never seen anything like it. When the rock landed in shallow water, the dog felt for it first with its front feet before plunging its head underwater to retrieve it. But when it went far enough out, the dog disappeared completely, sometimes being gone so long I was sure it must have drowned. Always it would come up again, rock between its teeth, and swim to shore, pausing as it came, to clear its ears.

"Does he ever miss?" I asked the man finally.

He turned, apparently noticing me for the first time. "She," he said. "Springer spaniel. Name's Lydia."

"Oh. Does *she* ever miss?"

He nodded. "Sometimes. But she almost always comes up with something. If she can't find the rock I threw, she finds another." He threw the rock again and the dog plunged into the water. "Once I threw a rock and she brought back a wallet. Empty. I told her she should find a full one next time, but she went back to rocks after that. Except for the time she tried to bring up a bike tire. That one almost did her in. She finally had to let it go."

"How'd you teach her to dive?"

"Didn't. I was skipping stones one day when she was still a pup, and she went after one. Thought I'd lost her for sure. But she got it. She's been diving ever since."

"Was that here?"

The man shook his head. "Upstate New York."

I glanced at my watch. I had to go if I was going to get my shower before supper, but I hated to leave while the dog was still diving. "Will you be coming back here sometime? Throwing rocks for her again?"

For a moment, the man's face changed. His eyes seemed to go dark, like a light had gone out. Then he nodded. "Same time, same place. Every day."

I grinned. "I'll see you again, then," I said. "You and Lydia."

Lydia barked and the man leaned down to pick up the rock, brushing water droplets from his jeans where she'd shaken all over his legs again. "Highly likely."

CHAPTER FOUR

Everybody who usually comes to Wednesday night prayer service had gathered in the church. There weren't many—around twenty people—but more than enough for me. Mrs. Quigley, in the dark red dress she wears like a go-to-church uniform, was sitting in the front row as always, next to Johnna. Behind them sat Elbert Hode, in his stained and holey work overalls, with Mrs. Hode, who always looks as if she just woke up from a really sound sleep, her eyes all squinty and unfocused. The Dirkman family with all five kids and the Schmidts with their four took up the next rows, and Miss Kunkle, the lady who owns so many cats that the town keeps wanting to take them away from her, sat at the far back. Dad says she sits at the back so she can be ready to hightail it home in case there's some kind of cat emergency. In front of her were the Johnsons, with their brand-new baby, our only African-American family. Our congregation is a pretty varied lot, but the one thing they tend to have in common is not a whole lot of money. If they had money, they'd be dressing up and going to St. John's Episcopal three blocks over, or First Presbyterian on Market Street. Of course, neither of those churches has Wednesday evening prayer services. So if our people had money, they'd be someplace else altogether. Mom says Dad has a loyal flock, but she wishes sometimes they had just a little more fleece to share.

Mom was playing the piano, as she always does, and Dad stood at the pulpit in his navy blue suit, waiting for the Dirkman kids to be shushed and get settled. Matthew and I, in our blue choir robes, were sitting on the bench where we always sit, a few feet from the altar. We had both gone to the bathroom before we left the house (our house is right next door to the church), but I was wishing I could go back there and lock myself in.

As Mom finished the hymn she was playing, Dad cleared his throat. "We have a splendid surprise this evening," he said. I noticed an incredible amount of dust swirling in the orange light from the setting sun that was coming in the side window and slanting across the worn carpet of the front aisle. "Matthew and Mark are going to preach for us."

Carolyn Dirkman, who's a year ahead of us in school, groaned and her mother flipped her in the back of the head.

Dad grinned. "I think the boys may feel like

agreeing with you just about now, Carolyn," he said, and Mrs. Dirkman flipped her again. "But I'm sure they'll do a wonderful job. After all, this is the moment they've been preparing for all their lives. And I know that while we all share this important event together, you'll be just as quiet and attentive"—he stared hard at Johnny, the Schmidts' six-year-old—"as you always are for me. But for now, let's begin as we always do, with the Lord's Prayer. After that, we'll sing number two thirty-four in your hymnals, 'Washed in the Blood of the Lamb.'"

We bowed our heads and closed our eyes. I could hear Matthew's and my voices saying the prayer along with everybody else, but I figured it must be the twin thing making my mouth work, because my head had gone off somewhere else. For some reason, when I closed my eyes I saw that dog diving for rocks. I could see the sun on the water and her stub of a tail circling like a little propeller as she went down. I wished that when I opened my eyes I'd be back at the park, sitting by the lake. I kept my eyes closed after the "Amen" as Mom started the introduction to the hymn, till Matthew jabbed his elbow into my side as he stood up. I opened my eyes and stood up with him, taking my side of the open hymnbook. I could feel the pages quivering, not just on my side but on Matthew's, too. We had twin shakes, and somehow that made me feel just the littlest bit better.

We sang. Dad read the Bible verses we were using

as the basis for our sermon. He asked the kids to come up front for their blessing. And he took a little longer with his hand on Johnny Schmidt's head as Johnny kicked at the base of the pulpit. Johnny squirmed a little, but he stopped kicking. Dad asked the congregation to give the names of the people they wanted prayers for, and then he prayed, naming all those people and mentioning what they needed, and then running down his usual list of impossible things—world peace, the healing of the environment, the integrity of politicians, an end to starvation, racial harmony, and "light in the general darkness." And then he added a prayer for Matthew and me "as they embark on a journey that will, we all hope, lead to a life of commitment to your work in the world."

Mom played the Doxology then, and Luke and Johnna came up to the front to get the collection plates that they were passing, since Matthew and I had this other job tonight—this preaching job. As soon as the collection plates had gone up on the altar, it would be time for us to begin. I swallowed around what felt like a rock stuck in my throat. What if, when I went to speak, no sound would come out?

And then Mom finished playing and it was time. Dad left the pulpit and sat down on the chair behind it, and I felt Matthew stand up from our bench. I watched him, like watching myself, walk to the pulpit, the sleeves of his robe quivering as he went. "Take your time," Dad had told us when we practiced just before dinner. "Don't let yourself get rushed. Establish eye contact with your congregation before you begin."

Matthew laid his little pile of note cards on the pulpit, took a deep breath I could feel in my own lungs, and grabbed hold of the pulpit's sides as if it was the only thing floating in an endless ocean and he was about to drown. He cleared his throat. Involuntarily, I cleared mine, too. The rock was still there, its edges sharp. "'Ask, and it shall be given you,'" he said, his voice squeaking a little. He cleared his throat again. "That's what the Bible promises. That's what prayer is all about. Us asking for what we need. It's important to know that every one of us who believes in Jesus can just kneel down anytime we feel the need and ask him for help. And he'll give it to us. Every single time. 'Seek, and ye shall find.' We know that Jesus won't let us stray, like lost lambs, and . . . and . . ." Matthew looked down at his pile of cards. He forgot about holding on to the pulpit and began shuffling his cards. He must have put them upside down, I thought. Upside down and backward. I checked the pile of cards in my own sleeve to be sure they were right side up, my fingers feeling cold and damp.

"Like lost lambs," Matthew repeated as he found the card he was looking for. "Because we have only to seek him and we will find our way again. We have only to knock and his door will open to us. . . ."

I stopped listening and began going over my part

in my mind. And then, suddenly, Matthew was sitting down next to me. He punched me in the side. Someone out in the congregation giggled and someone made shushing noises. I stood up. My fingers had gone numb, and the cards I was clutching fell out of my sleeve and scattered across the rug. There was a ripple of laughter—not quiet little giggles, but real laughter—while I scrambled to pick up my cards. It would take forever to get them back in order, so I just jammed them together in a wad. When I had them all, I went to stand up, stepped on the hem of my robe, and very nearly pitched myself headfirst down the two steps into the aisle. Now even the people who had managed, out of politeness, not to laugh at me before joined the others. Johnna was practically doubled over in the front row, laughing so hard she looked about to fall out of the pew. For a fifth grader, she can be pretty immature sometimes. Mrs. Quigley had a hand on her back, but she was laughing, too. It was just like my nightmare.

Somehow I got to the pulpit, dropped the wad of cards, swallowed around the rock in my throat, and looked out at the people who were struggling to stop laughing. Luke made a face at me, and Johnny Schmidt, whose older brother had just whacked him on the shoulder to make him stop laughing, whacked his brother back. I glanced sideways at Dad. His face was so carefully serious that I knew he was having to bite the insides of his cheeks to stay that way. He gave me a thumbs-up.

I took the deep breath I was supposed to take and tried to remember my first words. "'C-c-consider the lilies of the field,'" I said, my voice shaking. Then I remembered about keeping eye contact. I looked right into Elbert Hode's eyes and the rest of my verse just vanished from my mind. I was a total blank. The cards were so scrambled, they wouldn't do me any good. Please, God, I thought desperately as I saw Carolyn Dirkman roll her eyes toward the ceiling. *Please!* Time seemed to stop, and Mrs. Schmidt reached over in slow motion to stop Johnny from whacking his brother again. Suddenly, the words were there in my mind.

"'Consider the lilies of the field, how they grow—'" My voice had settled down a little. It was still quivery, but not so bad. "'They toil not, neither do they spin: And yet I say unto you, That even Solomon in all his glory was not arrayed like one of these.'" I swallowed again; the rock had vanished. "What Matthew was just telling us is exactly right. We who believe in the Lord Jesus Christ have only to ask for what we need and we will surely be given it. But the true story, the good news of the Gospel, is that it's even better than that! Just like Jesus said. Consider the lilies. Lilies, like people, have needs. You all know daylilies—those beautiful orange flowers we see every summer growing all over Ohio, along roads and next to fields and up against fences, where there's no gardener to take care of them. They need sun and rain and nourishment. But they *can't* ask for those things. Do they still get what they need? Out there where there's no sprinkler to water them and nobody to put fertilizer down around their roots?" Dad had told me to pause, but I would probably have forgotten if I hadn't needed to take a breath. I felt like I'd been running.

"I ask you," I said then. "Does anyone here remember a summer when there were no daylilies in Ohio?" Mrs. Quigley shook her head. "Do you remember a summer without grass?"

"A good thing," Elbert Hode called out. "If there was no grass, there'd be no need to hire me to cut it!" Everybody laughed again.

People didn't usually interrupt Dad's sermons, but I figured it was a good thing to be interrupted. At least it meant somebody was listening. I just nodded my head and kept going, so I wouldn't forget what came next. Elbert had started something, though. During the next part, Mrs. Johnson said "Amen" once and "Tell it, Mark" another time. Finally, I got to the last part. "The lilies and the grass don't have to pray for what they need. They just get it. Jesus told us that we don't have to, either. 'For your heavenly Father knoweth that ye have need of all these things.' Jesus said that to worry about where your next meal is coming from or whether you'll have clothes on your back is to be without faith. Not to trust in God. So—if there is something you need, it's okay to get down on your knees and pray for it. But even if you don't, God knows exactly what it is you need, and if you have faith, he will see that you get it! 'Take therefore no thought for the morrow, for the morrow shall take thought for the things of itself.'"

I was done. Now that it was over, it seemed to have gone very fast. I ducked my head a little, as Dad had told me to. Like taking a bow, only there wouldn't be any applause. I didn't need applause. I was just so glad to be finished, I could hardly walk back to sit down next to Matthew. It was over. I'd done it! *We* had done it! Preached our first sermon. No wonder this wasn't Dad's favorite part of being a minister. I had to pee again, and I wasn't sure my dinner wasn't going to come back up. But it was over. I heard Dad's voice announce the final hymn and Mom begin to play it.

When the service was over, we followed Dad to the door into the big classroom. We stood with him as the congregation filed past and shook our hands. Then we all went in for refreshments—punch for the kids and coffee for the grown-ups and Mrs. Quigley's lemon bars for everybody.

Matthew and I stood together near the refreshment table. There were lots of congratulations, but I was so relieved just to have survived the whole thing that I didn't really listen. I figured people were just being polite, anyway. But then, chomping on a lemon bar, Carolyn Dirkman came up to us and waved her punch glass. "You guys don't really believe all that, do you? All that 'ask, and ye shall receive' and 'lilies of the field' stuff."

We nodded. "It's right there in the Bible," Matthew said about half a second before I would have said the same thing.

"Oh, sure," she said. "Then how come there are homeless people? And what about fires?"

"Fires?" I couldn't figure out what she was talking about.

"Yeah, fires. People get burned out and lose everything, and not everybody has your father and his church to bring them old clothes and blankets and food and stuff. Some people *die* in fires! Even good people who pray like crazy to get rescued. So how does that fit with God giving people what they ask for, or knowing what people need and giving it to them? And what about brush fires? You think daylilies and grass wouldn't get burned up if there was a brush fire? It doesn't make any sense, about God knowing what we need and just giving it to us. If he did, nothing really, really bad would ever happen. Nobody would be poor. Nobody would get sick. Nobody would die."

She gulped the rest of her punch and went to the other end of the table to get another glass. We stood there, looking after her. Matthew shrugged. "She just doesn't get it."

"Yeah," I said. "O ye of little faith."

CHAPTER FIVE

After the prayer service we went up to our room, and Matthew sat at the desk to do his math homework. In my worry about the prayer service, I'd forgotten to take my backpack to soccer practice with me, so I didn't have my book and notebook at home. I would just have to punt the next day.

I had the book I was reading for my language arts book report, though. I found it and sat down on my bed. But I couldn't concentrate. I was reading words, but nothing was sticking in my head. I kept thinking about the service, going over and over what we'd said and wishing we'd done it differently. Trying to think of some way we could have said it so that Carolyn Dirkman wouldn't have argued about it afterward. What had we left out?

"So—what'd you think?" Matthew said. He was turned around in the chair, his back to the desk, so I guessed he wasn't being able to concentrate, either. "We did okay, didn't we? They actually listened."

I shrugged. "Dad says we did good."

Matthew shook his head and rubbed at the back of his neck. "I think we went too fast. It took five minutes in practice, with Dad reminding us all the time to pause, but for real, I think it took about three. We need to do it more. Do you suppose Dad'll let us preach again next week?"

I shook my head. "He can't have us doing the prayer service every week. People would stop coming."

"Not if we got good at it!"

"I don't think I'll ever get good at it," I said. "Did you hear my voice shaking?" Matthew nodded. "I'm not hot to do it again anytime soon. I've never been so scared in my life!"

Matthew grinned. "I was scared, too. My hands were shaking so hard I couldn't even hold my cards. But that's because it was the first time. You remember our first soccer practice? In third grade? We couldn't even kick the ball when the coach sent it straight to us. And when you tried to get the ball from Zach you fell smack on your butt and missed it completely."

"Thanks for reminding me," I said. I still remembered the feel of my foot skipping off the top of the ball and me flopping down backward. Everybody there, including Matthew, had laughed.

"But that was five years ago. And look at us now! We're two of the best players on the team. People aren't any good at something the first time they try it. You have to practice. I'm going to ask Dad if we can't start preaching regularly. Not every week, but once a month maybe. You've seen kid preachers on TV. And Dad says Uncle T.T. started regular preaching, Sunday preaching even, when he was twelve."

"Yeah, but Uncle T.T. was some kind of prodigy. He was the one in his generation with the gift. We don't have it."

"Who says?"

I just shook my head. "*I* say! According to Dad, the very first time Uncle T.T. preached, he talked for half an hour and four people came to the front of the church to be saved. No point trying to pretend we're like that!"

Matthew shrugged. "Okay, but Dad's a good preacher, even without the gift. He must have had to practice. That's all we need. The more we do it, the better we'll get. And we won't be so nervous next time."

Matthew was right, and I knew it. I could tell by the glint in his eyes that he was as excited about preaching as he'd ever been about anything. After all, it was what we'd been told our whole lives that we'd do someday. What we'd always *wanted* to do! Take the Word of God to people. Somewhere in me was the same excitement Matthew was feeling. It was what kept me from being able to concentrate on my book.

But seeing that glint in his eye did something to that feeling. Like putting wet leaves on a campfire.

We were supposed to be God's instruments—twin preachers. I'd known that all my life. But was *I*? Me, separately—Mark Thomas Filkins?

"Ask him if you want, but just ask him for yourself," I said. "I don't want to preach again right now. Not for a long, long time!" I picked up my book.

Matthew nodded. "Okay. But you'll change your mind, you'll see. Once you get over remembering how nervous you were tonight."

Was he right? Would I change my mind? I picked up my book and tried reading again. And felt as if the wet leaves had put the fire out completely. Instead of seeing the words on the pages, I was seeing images of Matthew and me: running down the soccer field, passing the ball back and forth between us with perfect timing. Standing at the counter at the drugstore, choosing candy bars and knowing that whichever one one of us chose the other would like, knowing that we'd split them with each other. Racing each other on either side of a car at a church fund-raising car wash, and meeting at almost exactly the same moment in the center of the front bumper. The time we dressed alike on school picture day and the photographer had sent me away, saying nobody was allowed to get his picture taken twice. Those had been the images of my whole life. Good images. They didn't feel so good anymore.

Later, when Luke came up and the three of us knelt down to say our prayers, I said the aloud part with the others, but then I focused my mind on Jesus and continued my prayer just inside my head.

Something's wrong with me, I told him, and I don't know what it is. I hope you'll make it go away. Or at least help me with it. I've never felt anything like this before, and it sort of scares me. I didn't get any answer, of course. "That's what faith is all about," Dad had told us often enough. You don't have to have the answers carved in stone like Moses with the Ten Commandments. You just have to trust that they'll come.

Faith. Just because Carolyn Dirkman didn't get it didn't mean it didn't work. I had faith all right. All the Filkinses do. Later, as I was going to sleep, instead of letting my mind give me any old memories or images it felt like giving me, I purposely imagined a great big clump of orange daylilies.

CHAPTER SIX

When we got down for breakfast the next morning, Dad was doing toast-watch duty (our toaster oven turns everything to charcoal if you turn your back on it for a second), Johnna was at the table spooning cereal into her mouth, and Mom was reading the paper. Luke wasn't down yet because we'd managed to get into the bathroom before him for a change. I pointed to the toaster and put up two fingers to let Dad know I wanted two pieces of toast instead of my usual one. For some reason I was starving, maybe because I'd been running in my dreams all night. Around and around the soccer field. Racing against something that was always getting ahead of me.

"What's a noble lariat?" Johnna asked around a mouthful of Cheerios.

"A what?" Mom asked from behind the paper.

"A noble lariat . . ."

Luke came in and dropped his books on the

counter. "I know! A cowboy's virtuous rope," he said as he plopped into his chair.

Mom put the paper down. "What are you talking about?"

Johnna pointed. "On the front page. It says there's a noble—"

"No*bel.*" Dad said. "A Nobel laureate. Someone who's won a Nobel Prize."

"Noble lariat!" Matthew nearly spit orange juice on the table, laughing.

Johnna, her face red, aimed a kick at him under the table.

"Someone in *Bradyville* won a Nobel Prize?" Luke asked as he emptied the last of the Cheerios into his bowl. "Are they kidding?"

"Don't you remember all that fuss a couple years ago?" Matthew said. "He's Bradyville's one and only claim to fame."

"What's the Nobel Prize *for*?" Johnna asked. "I bet you don't know," she said to Matthew.

"Medicine," Matthew said.

"That's one," Dad said. "Also chemistry and physics—"

"Don't forget economics," Mom said.

Dad grinned. "How could I forget economics?"

Mom is the one in the family who thinks about money. Dad just mostly spends it. Not on us so much as on others—people who need it more, he says. Even though they both have part-time jobs to bring in extra money, he and Mom argue about it a lot.

"Is there money with the prize?" I asked. "Or is it just the honor?"

"There's money," Mom said. "Usually around a million dollars, I think."

Matthew whistled. "Like winning the lottery."

"That's probably what it feels like to win," Dad said.

"So it's big money for doing science," Luke said.

"Not just science. There's a prize for literature, too. And the one I think is most important—the Peace Prize. That's given to the person who has done the most for world peace."

"Jesus should have won that one," Johnna said.

"If there'd been such a thing back then, he probably would have," Dad said.

"Is that what the Bradyville guy won for?" Luke asked. "Peace?"

Mom turned to the front page of the paper and read aloud the headline Johnna had seen. "'Nobel laureate returns to Bradyville.'" Then she began reading the article as Dad tossed pieces of toast to Matthew and me across the table. "'Dr. Colin Hendrick, forty-nine, our own Nobel laureate, has come home to Bradyville. He is staying for an unspecified length of time with his father, Robert Arthur Hendrick, M.D., eighty-four, who retired last year after fifty-five years of family practice. Hendrick, world-famous for more than two decades of work with genetic engineering, was granted the Nobel Prize two years ago for breakthrough research.

Hendrick found a way to transfer genes from oil-eating bacteria to the life-forms indigenous to any aquatic environment. The organisms, newly engineered to consume oil, can live in natural conditions wherever an oil spill occurs, and because they break the oil down in normal metabolic processes, there is no residue from the cleanup process that could do further environmental damage. "There need never again be an environmental disaster on the scale of the *Exxon Valdez,*" Hendrick was quoted as saying when his method was shown to be successful.'"

Dad shook his head as he put fresh slices of bread into the toaster oven. "Will we never learn?"

"What do you mean?" Luke asked. "Learn what?"

"Not to interfere with God's plan. Genetic engineering! Just because scientists *can* do something doesn't mean they should! The creation of life is God's job, not ours."

"Sounds like what he's doing's a good thing," Luke said. "Cleaning up oil spills."

"We don't know enough," Mom said, "to know what's a good thing and what isn't."

Johnna looked at Mom, her eyes full of objections. "*I* do. There was a picture in our news magazine at school of dead birds on a beach, all coated with black gunk. It was awful. It made me want to cry. *That's* not a good thing."

Mom sighed. "You're right. It's not good for birds to die because of an oil spill. But maybe what this man wants us to do to clean it up will turn out someday to be worse."

"But they said—," Luke began.

Dad overrode him. "Genetic engineering changes life itself. And there's no way to know where that can lead."

"Well, anyway," Matthew said, "it's pretty neat that somebody that famous is actually here in Bradyville. Does it say why he came home?"

Mom scanned the rest of the article. "Not really. As old as the father is, it could be that he's sick and needs a little extra care and attention. I don't suppose a scientist as busy as Colin Hendrick can be away from his work for very long. His lab is in upstate New York, and this says he's in the middle of further critical research."

"More of the same? Genetic engineering?"

Mom nodded.

"Coincidence," Matthew said. "Mrs. Gerston's bringing some science guy to our science class starting next week to do some extra stuff with us."

I'd been thinking the same thing. I looked at the picture that went with the article. It showed a smiling dark-haired man in a tuxedo standing at a podium. The caption said it had been taken at the awards ceremony. "Maybe it's him," I said.

"Oh, sure," Luke scoffed. "A Nobel laureate teaching an eighth-grade science class. That'd be like Pelé coming to coach your soccer team!"

"Who's Pelé?" Johnna asked.

"He won the Nobel Prize of soccer," Matthew said.

"All right, you guys, stop teasing!"

After soccer practice that afternoon, when everybody was heading home, I told Matthew I wanted to go for a walk by the lake. He said he guessed that would be okay, but he had some stuff he wanted to do before dinner, so we shouldn't stay too long.

"Why don't you go ahead, then," I said. "I'll see you later."

He just looked at me. I could see it took a minute for him to get what I'd said. "You mean you want to walk by the lake by *yourself*?"

I nodded. He stood for a minute, changing his backpack from one hand to the other, his/my face all open and surprised. "Something wrong?" he asked finally.

"Nope." At least not anything I could explain.

He shrugged and put on his backpack. "Okay, then." He started away, then turned back. "It's our turn to set the table, remember. So don't be late."

CHAPTER SEVEN

I sat for a while on the bench near the willow, not thinking, just watching the way the wind made patterns on the water. They kept changing, so the lake looked different from one minute to the next. A couple of birds swooped across, dipping their beaks into the water and changing the wind pattern even more.

Coach MacMahon had put Matthew with Zach for passing practice and me with Colby Gaston. I'd fallen completely apart. When I tried to pass, it always went either so far in front of him that he couldn't get to it or completely behind him. With Matthew I always had a sense of where he'd be, so I didn't have to plan where I was passing. We ran together and sent the ball back and forth between us—that was all. Like tossing a ball from one hand to the other—you don't have to think; you just do it. I'd always thought we were such good passers. Coach always said we were. But now I knew it was only the twin thing again. If we started playing on different teams, maybe I'd have to learn how to play soccer all over again. I didn't see how Matthew and Zach were doing, because they were at the other end of the field. I didn't know whether I really wanted to know or not. I felt like there was a wind blowing in my life, changing the patterns in a way I couldn't control.

Suddenly a brown-and-white shape came hurtling around the bench and the dog from yesterday was greeting me, wagging her stump of a tail and quivering all over, her ears pricked up and what looked like a smile on her face. I reached out to her, and she licked my hand.

"That's pretty unusual," a voice said from behind me. I turned and looked up at the man, who was dressed as he had been the day before, in a red plaid shirt and jeans that were sort of gathered around the belt at his waist, as if he'd borrowed them from somebody a size bigger. "She doesn't usually take to strangers. You have a dog she might be smelling on your clothes?"

I shook my head. "We can't have pets," I said.

"Allergies in the family?" he asked.

"Not in the family. My dad's a minister and he takes in people sometimes. People who don't have anyplace else to go. He says it would be selfish to have pets. We might have to turn away somebody in need just because they were allergic."

I rubbed Lydia's ears, pleased to think she'd

come to me even though she didn't usually like strangers. I'd always wanted a dog. When Matthew and I were little, we'd had a really big black dog named Prince and a monkey named Mr. Teedle. Both of them were imaginary. I made up Prince, and Matthew made up Mr. Teedle.

"Mind if I join you?"

I shook my head and the man lowered himself sort of stiffly onto the other end of the bench. Lydia pulled away from me, went over to him, and started jumping around, barking.

He just shook his head. "Leave it alone awhile, would you? I just sat down."

"Would it be okay if I threw a rock for her?" I asked.

"Sure. Just don't make it too big. The dog has no sense at all—if you threw in an anvil she'd drown herself trying to bring it up."

She seemed to me to have lots of sense. The minute I stood up from the bench she started frisking around me, stubby tail circling, as if she'd understood exactly what I'd said to the man. I found a rock about the size of my fist and tossed it a little way into the water. It was too close. She found it with her front paws and barely had to duck her head to retrieve it.

"Tell her to bring it to you," the man said.

"Bring it here, Lydia," I told her. She looked at me and shook her head, water flying off the tips of her ears, then bounded off along the lake's edge. When she got about ten feet away, she turned and ran in a huge half circle around me and then back again. "Lydia!" I called. "Bring it to me!"

She looked over at the man, and he nodded at her. "Take him the rock!"

And, just like that, she brought it and laid it down at my feet. Then she backed off and barked. This time I threw it far. And this time she really had to dive for it. It blew me away all over again, watching her paddle out to the center of the circle the ripples were making, duck her head down so that only her rear end was showing, and then disappear completely. Like a seal. Like human pearl divers I'd seen on a PBS documentary. It seemed like some kind of miracle, a dog doing this.

This time the man didn't have to tell her to bring it to me. She shook herself all over and brought the rock and sat directly in front of me, still holding it in her mouth. I held out my hand and she laid it on my open palm and then started frisking and barking. I threw it again; she brought it to me again. Over and over she brought it back, no matter how close or how far I threw it. It was the same rock she brought, too. Every time.

"Time to quit," the man said finally. "She has no sense, I tell you. She'd go on diving if you kept it up till dark. Come on, Lydia. Enough."

I took the rock back to the bench. "Better hang

on to it," he said. "If you put it on the ground, she'll just pick it up and bring it to one of us and beg. I haven't the energy to take a stand against those eyes."

I looked at Lydia, who was sitting in front of me gazing up at me, expectantly. The fur around both of her eyes was reddish brown, but she had a patch of white on her head that became a stripe down between her eyes and then spread out across her whole muzzle, as if white paint had been poured on her head and had run down between her eyes. Around her brown nose there were a few spots of brown in the white fur, like freckles. Her long, silky ears, still dripping with water, in spite of her last hard shake, were red-brown, and so was her back. Her dark eyes looked up at me from beneath red-brown eyebrows, in a way that could melt the hardest heart. Come on, come on, *pl-ee-ee-a-s-e*! they were saying.

"No more," I said, and slipped the rock into my backpack. She watched me awhile longer, then went back down to the edge of the lake. She turned back to give me another pleading look. "No!" I said. After a moment she went off along the water's edge, sniffing at the ground, as if to say she could find her own entertainment if she had to.

"Some dog!" I said to the man.

He didn't answer at first. Just sat there, watching her, tapping the fingers of one thin hand against his knee. "She's ten years old," he said finally. "You'd never know it to look at her. Or to watch her dive. Getting to be an old lady."

"Does that mean she's seventy?" I asked, remembering that dogs were supposed to age seven years for every one of ours.

"Not exactly," he said. "It goes much faster than seven to one at first, but then it sort of plateaus. A dog's a grown-up for a very long time before it gets old. But then things speed up again. I doubt that she'll be diving like that much longer."

We both sat for a while watching Lydia sniff her way along a waterlogged tree limb that must have washed ashore from the nature preserve on the other side of the lake. The man sighed. "She's starting to slow down some. She'll sleep when we get home, and then when she wakes up, she'll limp awhile. She gets stiff after a session like this. Arthritis. Strange," he added under his breath, so I could hardly make out the word.

"What's strange?" I asked, not sure he had meant me to hear.

"Oh, nothing. Just that I almost didn't get another dog after my last one. She was a springer, too. Got sick. I had to have her put down, and I told myself I didn't want to go through that again. Dogs don't live long enough. You have to keep saying good-bye. I didn't want to say good-bye again."

"But you got Lydia anyway?"

"Turns out I can't live without a dog," he said. "My life's not like your dad's."

"My dad's?"

"You said he's a minister, right? So he's got his congregation. And his family. You and . . . ?"

"Two brothers and a sister." I didn't say the word *twin*.

He shook his head. "Lydia's been my family. My reason to go home at night. Everybody needs to have a reason to go home at night. . . ."

After she finished going over every inch of the tree limb, Lydia came back over and sat herself directly between us, looking hopefully from one to the other. The man just shook his head. So I followed his example and shook mine. She watched us awhile longer, her big, soft, pleading eyes making me long to reach into my backpack and pull the rock out again. But I didn't want her to wear herself out too much, to make her arthritis worse. Finally, she gave up and lay down, her freckled white nose on her freckled white paws.

I don't usually talk to strangers. In fact, I don't remember ever even meeting a stranger without Matthew with me. And then the talk always got started, if it did at all, because we were twins. I'd never realized before how totally the world has related to us that way. As twins. But now, it was Lydia that the man and I talked about. How she was a Welsh springer, not English. A rarer breed. How he got her when she was just eight weeks old, not much more than a handful. And then we talked about soccer. And then school. Nothing serious. Nothing personal. Just talk. Just something to say because we were sharing a bench, looking at the same lake. And then we talked some about the lake. Only he called it a pond. About the fish it was stocked with, and all the other creatures who lived in it, and the reason swimming wasn't allowed. "Too many people," the man said. "Better to keep the people at the Y pool with the filter. And the chlorine. Better for them, and better for the pond as well."

And then I said I had to be getting home. "It's my turn to set the table." I'd almost said "our turn," but I caught myself in time. In all our talk, Matthew had never once come up. The man stretched his arms up over his head, and Lydia sat up, watching him. "She sure is tuned in to you," I said.

He nodded. "I'm all the family she's got, too," he said. As we'd talked, his voice had been light. But now there was something dark in it. Like there was something sad between him and Lydia. Between them and the world. I felt that sadness come over me, too, suddenly. As if I'd caught it from him. I wanted to be home in the bright kitchen then, where Luke and Johnna would probably be teasing each other and Matthew would be grumping about how late I was, and Mom would be stirring a big pot of stew or soup or spaghetti sauce or something that smelled good.

But then the man reached down to scratch Lydia's ears; her tail started its circles, and he smiled. "Bring the rock back next time you come. If we're here, she'll want to go diving some more. She'll know you."

"Okay," I said, and felt my heart lift. The sadness was gone as quickly as it had come. This dog would know me. Me, Mark. Not me, half a set of twins. I stood up and put on my backpack. Then I reached down and petted Lydia's cinnamon-colored back. "You're a good girl!" I told her. She grinned up at me. "I'll see you next time."

As I left the park, I knew I'd come back to the lake—the pond—after our next soccer practice. And maybe, since that wasn't till Monday, I'd come back here just to see if they were here. "Same time, same place," he'd said before. I just might be here, too, I thought. To throw the rock a little. And watch the miracle dog, who would know me, dive.

CHAPTER EIGHT

"Are you mad at me?" Matthew asked me the next morning as we were getting dressed.

I felt a twinge in my stomach. "What would I be mad about?"

"That's what I've been trying to figure out."

"Well, I'm not mad."

Matthew pulled on a faded red turtleneck and ran a hand through his hair to make his cowlick lie down. Mine—same side—was still standing up. "Then what's the matter?"

I concentrated on pulling on my socks, avoiding his eyes. "Nothing's the matter."

"This is me," he said. "It's like the toothpaste cap. You can't fool me."

We'd been playing the toothpaste cap game since summer. Whoever used the toothpaste first would hide the cap somewhere in the bathroom. The game started between Matthew and me, but it was Luke we drove crazy with it, because if he went to use the toothpaste in between us, he could never find it. The thing was, no matter which of us hid it and which of us went looking, we *could.* Every time. When Matthew hid it, I just had to close my eyes for a second and I could go right to it. Even the time he took the lid off the toilet tank and balanced the cap on the flushing assembly inside. When I hid it, he could do the same thing. At first we kept the game going to see if one of us could figure out a way to fool the other. When that didn't happen, we kept the game going just for the fun of it. It was weird, but it was kind of neat, too. Besides, we sort of liked driving Luke crazy.

I knew Matthew was right. Even if I could act exactly the same as usual, he would know that things weren't usual at all. I looked up and saw the hurt in his eyes. And then—for some reason—I *did* get mad.

For all my nearly fourteen years, I had been half of Matthew-Mark. How come all of a sudden I was feeling something he wasn't? Why didn't he have the same snake in the stomach that I had?

"I don't want to talk about it," I said.

He just stood there staring at me. I couldn't look anywhere except into those eyes that were my eyes. Except for that hurt look. His voice was low. "You're sure you're not mad?"

"I told you, didn't I? I'm not mad!" Except, of course, that now I was. "*I* wanted to wear red today," I said, wishing something that simple really was what was bugging me.

Matthew shrugged and pulled off his shirt, which made his cowlick stand up again. "So wear red. Big deal. I don't care!" He threw the shirt on his bed, grabbed a blue-and-white-striped one out of his dresser drawer, and went off to the bathroom, leaving me staring into the mirror. The real mirror, with just my own scowling face.

All through the school day, Matthew and I avoided each other. "What's up with you two?" Evan Elsasser asked at lunch, when we didn't eat our sandwiches and carrot sticks together. "You have a fight?"

"We don't fight," I told him.

"Yeah, well, you don't sit on opposite sides of the cafeteria, either."

"We do today."

As bad as I felt all day, watching Matthew making an effort to keep from even looking in my direction, there was something *not* bad about it, too. Just like when we were getting ready to do the sermon; the scared feeling, the shakes, the rock in my throat all making me miserable, but at the same time that edge of excitement from knowing that I was about to preach for the first time in my life. Hard to explain how I could be feeling both.

Mrs. Gerston was all bubbly with excitement when we came in to science class and settled at our desks. "Okay, gang—today's the day!" she said as she dragged the tall stool from its corner to the front of the classroom. She kept looking at the window in the door. "The visitor I promised you is coming to start a new unit with us. It's something the eighth grade has never studied quite like this before. At least I think it's safe to say that no eighth grade has ever had such a teacher before."

At that moment there was a knock at the door, and she pushed the hair back from her face, pulled her dress straight, and went to open it. "Class, I'd like you to welcome an old friend of mine—Dr. Colin Hendrick, Bradysville's Nobel Prize winner!" And she pushed open the door.

The man who came in was the man from the park. He was dressed just as he had been before, in baggy jeans and a plaid shirt. I blinked. Lydia's owner was the noble lariat? How could that be?

He didn't look anything like the picture in the newspaper. That guy had been wearing a tuxedo. He'd had shorter, darker hair, and he'd looked younger. He'd won the prize just two years ago, but that guy had looked much, *much* younger.

Everybody in the class except me was applauding. Brady Connor started stamping his feet and whistling. I was still swallowing my surprise.

Grinning like somebody who'd just taken Jesus as their personal savior, Mrs. Gerston led him to the stool at the front of the classroom. He looked out at the class and saw me. I started applauding with the others, hoping he hadn't noticed that I'd been sitting there like an idiot with my mouth hanging open and my hands in my lap. He smiled at me and I smiled back. Then he caught sight of Matthew, sitting in the next row. His eyebrows went up and he looked back at me, back at Matthew, and then back at me again. Then he shrugged just the tiniest little shrug and winked. Not at Matthew. At me! He'd recognized me! As Mrs. Gerston began talking and the applause dwindled down, I wondered, suddenly, if Lydia would be able to tell us apart. I'd never thought of that before. Did Matthew and I smell different enough for a dog to know which was which? I hoped so.

". . . in the same class from fourth grade all the way through high school graduation," Mrs. Gerston was saying. "By that time, he had already distinguished himself by winning the Westinghouse Science Award and had started on the path that he continues to travel to this day."

The class started applauding again, and this time I was right with them. I actually *knew* a Nobel laureate! I'd talked to him about soccer and school. I'd played with his dog. And he'd invited me to come back to the park and do it again! No wonder he'd known so much about the lake—the pond. I glanced sideways at Matthew. He was clapping like everybody else. He didn't suspect for a single minute that I knew anything more about Dr. Colin Hendrick than he did.

Dr. Hendrick held up his hands and the applause died down. He sat on the edge of the stool and smiled over at Mrs. Gerston, who was settling herself behind her desk. "Thank you, Virginia—Mrs. Gerston. Back in the eighth grade in this very school, I would never have imagined that one day I'd be a guest in your science class!" He looked back at the class and made a face. "I doubt that Miss Shreve, the meanest science teacher on four continents, would have imagined it, either. We sat at tables back then, in groups of six. Your teacher here, who had a very quick mind, had a habit of finishing her work ahead of everybody else—"

"Except you!" Mrs. Gerston said.

"And passing notes to one Carole Sue Munson, who sat across the table from her. From time to time, Miss Shreve caught her at it and sent her to the office."

"That's the trouble with a photographic memory," Mrs. Gerston said. "There are some things best forgotten."

"You heard her," he said. "Everyone in this room is to forget what I just told you. However, it's the last thing out of my mouth that you're allowed to forget, whether we're here in the classroom or out in the field. Okay?"

"In the field?" Denise Currier said. "What field? Where are we going?"

"That's one of the many mysteries we're going to explore in the next few weeks. I assume you've all heard of genetic engineering?" Everybody nodded.

"That's what they did in *Jurassic Park,*" Zach Soames said. "Like cloning."

Dr. Hendrick nodded. "Cloning is one kind of genetic engineering. How many of you know something about DNA?"

Only Todd Rathburn raised his hand this time. I sure didn't. I was afraid he might ask what it was, and I didn't really know, except that it had something to do with heredity and genes. Since Matthew and I came from the splitting of one fertilized egg, we had the same DNA and genes. It was what made us identical twins. Sort of natural clones. God's clones. But the truth was that I didn't even know *for sure* what genes and DNA were. They were just words I'd heard a lot in my life.

"We'll talk a little about these things, and what they may mean for the future of our planet. But we'll talk more about the planet itself and its life-forms. How many of you know what happens when an oil tanker goes down and spills its oil into the ocean?"

I don't think I remember an hour in a classroom my whole life that went as fast as the next one did, as Colin Hendrick described to us the oil spill in Beaver Creek that had started him on his scientific career. It had happened in the spring, when the creek was full of new life. He described the fish that died, their eggs destroyed, and the muskrats, the frogs and crayfish and insects. And the birds. The ducks that got oil on their feathers and tried to preen themselves clean and died of the poison of it. The baby ducks that got the heavy oil on their down and sank under the water and drowned. The baby raccoons that poisoned themselves eating oil-coated crayfish. By the time he finished talking about that oil spill, a couple of the girls were crying. He told them that he'd cried, too, even though he was a guy and a freshman in high school at the time. It was right then that he'd decided to spend his whole life trying to figure out how to keep that sort of thing from happening again. The next year he took first place in the science fair for a theory he had about the possibility of oil-eating bacteria. It was a much bigger, much longer experiment about oil-eating bacteria that made him first a finalist and then a winner of a Westinghouse scholarship.

Then he explained about what had won him the Nobel Prize—about how the organisms they genetically engineered in his lab were the organisms normal to the environment where the oil had been spilled. How they could be "seeded" on the spill and they'd start consuming the oil, reducing it to harmless elements, and then reproducing incredibly fast, and how while they lasted, other organisms could eat them. Instead of an environmental catastrophe that endangered all the forms of water and shore life, an oil spill could be turned into something at least a little bit positive, part of the food chain. For a little while.

As he talked, I kept hearing Dad's words in my head: "Just because scientists *can* do a thing doesn't mean they should!" It didn't seem to fit what Colin Hendrick had done. What could possibly be wrong with work that fixed a mess people had made? It was God's job to create, Dad had said. But God created Colin Hendrick, didn't he? God created this guy who cared so much about all those animals dying that he had to do something to keep it from happening again. It was God who gave Colin Hendrick the mind that let him think up a way to do that.

After school I couldn't keep avoiding Matthew. It wasn't a soccer-practice day, and there was no reason not to walk home together the way we always did. At first, neither of us said anything as we walked. Matthew was scuffling along the sidewalk, kicking at the odd pebble or stick that happened to get in his way.

"Dad's right, you know," he said finally. "People shouldn't mess around with life the way that guy's doing. Changing stuff and turning it loose in the world. Nobel Prize or not, it's not a good thing to do. What if those things he makes turn out to be poisonous? What if they turn out to be worse for the planet than the oil?"

"But they aren't poisonous!" I said. For some reason it felt like Matthew was attacking me instead of Colin Hendrick's work. "That's the whole point, the reason he got the prize! They eat the oil, and other things can eat them." I stopped and took a deep breath. "What he does doesn't hurt the planet; it helps it. He said so."

Matthew shook his head. "What if it takes a

really long time for the bad stuff about what he's doing to show up? Like that Agent Orange stuff they used in Vietnam. Maybe his engineered thingummies haven't been around long enough for us to know how bad they are. And maybe by the time we find out, it'll be too late, and the poison'll be in everything—like in the tuna fish Mom makes casseroles with. Uh-uh. Dad's right. People shouldn't try to do God's work."

"You know how Dad is always saying he's God's instrument, and that's what we should want to be, too? Well, why couldn't Colin Hendrick be God's instrument?"

"Colin Hendrick probably doesn't even believe in God."

"How do you know?"

"Because scientists don't! Because scientists think religion's nothing but ignorance and superstition."

"Not every scientist! Einstein believed in God," I said. I'd heard him quoted once—he said that God doesn't play dice with the universe. I figured he wouldn't have said that if he didn't believe in God.

"Yeah, well." Matthew turned toward me, and his face was set in a hard, angry frown. "It doesn't matter *what* a scientist thinks about God; genetic engineering is a bad thing!"

"Oil spills are a bad thing. And baby ducks drowning and their parents poisoning themselves trying to get clean. Those are bad things."

"Then it's God's job to take care of them. Not some scientist's."

"Yeah, well, I don't see God doing anything about oil spills. I haven't heard of any miraculous ocean cleanups! Jesus walking on the dirty water and the water getting all clean. Have you?"

He didn't answer. He just kept walking, faster and faster.

I didn't try to keep up. I stared at his back, at the jacket that was too small, so that his wrists stuck out from the sleeves, and the shoes that were worn down, so that his heels tipped in. My shoes were like that, too.

Lilies of the field, I thought. God was supposed to know what everyone and everything needed. Two days ago I would have agreed with everything Matthew had said. Now I didn't know.

Matthew turned around. "What *is* the matter with you? Come on!"

I stopped. "I'm going to the park," I said, looking past Matthew at the bush behind him that had a few leaves just starting to turn red. "By myself."

Matthew didn't say a word. He just turned back around and walked on toward home.

Fine, you just do that! See what I care. I thought the words he hadn't said. If he'd said them I could be mad at him. But he hadn't. He hadn't said anything.

I cut across the street and headed for the park.

CHAPTER NINE

He was there. Sitting on the bench, his elbows on his knees, looking down at the dirt between his feet. Lydia was there, too, sniffing along the water's edge. I hadn't really expected them to be there this time, as if Colin Hendrick's coming to our class had changed things, had taken him out of this world, where he was just some stranger who sort of knew me, and put him forever into the school world, where he was a famous scientist who was there for everybody. But I knew the minute I saw them how much I'd been hoping they'd be there.

"How'd you recognize me?" I asked him before I even got to the bench.

Colin Hendrick turned to look at me and Lydia came frisking up to be petted. "You didn't tell me you had a twin," he said, instead of answering my question.

"Nobody can ever tell us apart. So how did you?"

He smiled and pointed. "Your bracelet. Your brother wasn't wearing one."

"You remembered that?"

He nodded. "I notice details. It's a habit. And Ginny—Mrs. Gerston's right. I have a photographic memory. Once I see something, I tend to remember it."

I looked at the bracelet on my wrist, somehow disappointed. It was such a simple answer. What else had I expected? Lydia jumped up on me, nosing at my hands, as if I might be holding her rock. I knelt down by her and rubbed her ears.

"You didn't mention being a twin. . . ."

I started to say something, but he waved me quiet.

"Not that I think you *should* have. It was just surprising to see you apparently in two places at once."

I unzipped my pack and fished in the bottom for the rock. Lydia, as if she knew what I was doing, started barking. "Possess your soul in patience!" I told her, pushing books to one side. "I'm looking for it."

"'Possess your soul...'?" Colin Hendrick repeated.

I felt my cheeks getting warm. What a stupid thing to say. "It's from the Bible. It's what my mother always says when somebody's bugging her," I explained. Lydia had stopped barking now and was shoving her nose into my pack as if to help me find the rock. I shrugged. "Dogs don't have souls, of course."

"And humans do?" he said.

I looked up at him. "Well, *sure*!"

"Well, *sure,*" he repeated. Was he mocking me?

My hand had closed over the rock now, and I brought it out. Lydia went into her full frisking, begging mode. "May I throw it for her?"

"Well, *sure*!" he said again, and smiled. I smiled back, still not sure if he was mocking me or not, and threw the rock. Lydia took off into the water.

"You feel like helping me a little?" he asked as I stood and watched Lydia dive. "You can be my field assistant."

"Doing what?"

He reached into his bag and pulled out a couple of wide-mouthed plastic bottles. "Collecting some water samples. For your next science class."

"Water samples from here?"

He nodded. "Why not? It's water!"

"Yeah, but . . ."

"We don't have to go into the wilderness. Not that there's any left in Ohio anyway. There's plenty to learn from a pond in the middle of a park in the middle of town. I'll take the class on a couple of field trips later. For now we don't have to go farther than here. You can be my assistant for the field trips, too, if you want. The pay's lousy, but the hours are good."

Lydia came bounding up, dropped the rock at my feet, and shook herself, soaking my pants. I barely noticed. A Nobel Prize–winning scientist had asked me to be his field assistant. "Well, *sure*!"

His deep, hearty laugh surprised me. For that matter, he looked as if it had surprised him, too. I laughed with him and Lydia started barking.

I went around the edge of the pond to the reedy part and collected two plastic bottles full of water, fighting off Lydia, who wanted to snatch them out of my hands. Then I collected two more from the place closest to the bike trail, where there was a sort of beach area where kids waded sometimes and lots of people threw balls and sticks for their dogs to retrieve. In both places I scooped up a little of the bottom muck with the water, the way he'd told me to, then screwed the lids on tight. None of the bottles looked very promising—just some dirty water and some hairy-looking green weed.

When Colin Hendrick came to science class the next time, he brought one of the bottles of pond water I'd collected. Mrs. Gerston had put a binocular microscope on the lab table at the front of the class, and he set things up there. First he poured some of the pond water into a low white enamel pan, explaining as he did it where the water had come from. He talked for a while about how many life-forms there are all around us all the time that most of us don't notice or don't know about. Then he said the water had settled enough in the pan for us to see what he wanted us to see. We gathered around the table to look into the pan. "Look carefully, now. What do you see?"

"Dirty water," Brady Connor said. "And hairy green stuff."

But after a minute, Sophie Salten let out kind of a yelp. "There's a bunch of little things in there," she said. "Little live things."

Colin nodded. "Keep looking." He set a big rectangular magnifying glass down across the pan and had us take turns looking through it. I was probably more surprised than anybody at what I saw through that magnifying glass, because I'd gotten the water in the first place. And when I got it, I didn't see anything alive in it except the green stuff, which I knew had to be some kind of water plant. I figured the green proved it was alive—when a leaf or a blade of grass or something dies, it turns brown. But now I saw lots of teeny little specks swimming around in the water—like animated punctuation marks. Some swam sort of smoothly and some jerked from one place to another. Some were fast and some were slower, and tiny as they were, you could see they were different shapes. One of the jerky kinds had what looked like little fins on the back end—like a torpedo. Then, as I was staring at the little commas and periods swimming, I saw what looked like an eyelash that had fallen into the water—exactly as small and as thin as that. Just as I focused on it, it wiggled very fast and vanished into the green stuff.

I don't know why, but it made me feel really weird—I got chills. Nothing that looked like that eyelash should be able to move on its own!

Colin Hendrick explained that what we were looking at were zooplankton—copepods, and rotifers and worms—and that there are freshwater ones and saltwater ones and they can be found in most of the still waters in the world. "An old word for them that I particularly like is *animalcules,*" he said, "which means—appropriately enough—'little animals.'" He said there are all different kinds and they all have different names and different shapes. Some of them, like the daphnia, or water fleas, have hemoglobin in them just like our red blood cells and some of them have what look like rotating wheels that are really little hairs that move in waves around and around. Those are the rotifers. Lots of them are big enough to see with the naked eye or a good magnifying glass. But there are others that can be seen only with a microscope.

He sucked up a little water in an eyedropper and squeezed a drop onto a glass slide. "Anybody see anything here?" he asked, and showed the slide around so everybody got a chance to look at it. There were no little live things. Just a clear drop of water. Then he put a thin piece of glass down on the drop of water, put the slide under the microscope, and adjusted the mirror underneath to catch the light. "Now take a look."

We had to take turns. We could see more little

live things under the microscope. Some looked like little blobs of jelly that moved on their own, changing their shape as they went. Some had little moving hairs all around the edges, or a long tail that moved them through the water. All of them were transparent and you could see little dots and circles and spots in them. Some of the spots were sort of grayish and some were green or red.

"Eeeeuuuww, Dr. Hendrick!" Nicole Burbeck squealed when she looked into the microscope. "Are there things like this swimming around in our drinking water?"

"Not if the city treatment plant's doing its job," he said.

He explained that people used to think all living things were either plants or animals. Identifying them that way, some of the things we could see in the water would be classified as animals and some as plants, and some would be a sort of a combination—animals because they moved on their own, plants because they had chlorophyll and could make their own food out of sunlight and water. Because of those sorts of combinations, scientists had come up with five different classifications for living creatures now instead of just two, plant or animal.

What he wanted us all to know was that not just ducks and fish and clams and worms and cattails and lily pads lived in ponds and streams. There were all kinds of life-forms out there that were way too small for us to notice. And those were the kinds of life-forms that he worked with. Those were life-forms that were affected by the quality of the water first. "The world is a lot more complex than most people imagine."

"I saw this TV show," Todd Rathburn said, "that showed animals so small, you can't even see 'em with a regular microscope. Little bugs that live in the holes your eyelashes grow out of."

Nicole squealed again and put her hands over her eyes.

"Don't worry, mascara probably kills them," Sophie told her. Nicole wears more makeup than just about any girl in the whole school.

Colin Hendrick explained the difference between the microscope we were using and the electron microscopes that let people see the mites Todd was talking about. It was all about using beams of electrons instead of light, and I don't think anybody really understood him, except that electron microscopes were bigger and magnified things a whole lot more.

He told us we were going to go on a field trip to Beaver Creek, the place where the tanker truck had dumped its oil when he was in high school. He wanted us to see how many life-forms depended on the water in that system, how many life-forms were affected by an accident like that.

"How long ago was that oil spill?" Evan Elsasser asked.

"More than thirty years ago," Colin Hendrick answered.

"So there won't be any of that oil left, will there?"

"The creek will have recovered by now, but I'm not sure what we'll see when we get there. Nothing that happens is without its long-term effects, though they may be so small that we can't always be sure what they are. The main thing I want you all to be aware of, to remember, is that the water systems on our planet are vitally important to us. In some ways they are incredibly powerful systems and in other ways they're fragile—the systems and the life-forms that depend on them. When we damage them, we can't be sure what the results will be."

"There hasn't been another oil spill since back then, has there?" Todd Rathburn asked. "So the creek ought to be fine now."

Colin Hendrick shook his head. "It isn't just big noticeable accidents like oil spills—catastrophes—that have an effect on water systems. The greater danger is from ordinary daily things, from the way we live today. Fertilizer and pesticide runoff, dumping, leakage from gasoline storage tanks, that sort of thing. There's no way to know until we get out there how healthy Beaver Creek is now."

I thought of the Bible saying that man was to be the guardian of the earth, having dominion over the creatures. We weren't doing such a great job. I raised my hand.

"Mark?" Colin Hendrick said, and I could feel Matthew looking at me. He didn't know how Colin Hendrick knew my name.

"Can the work you do help with other problems besides oil spills? The other stuff that wrecks the water systems?"

"Good question. We're working, and other scientists are working, to see if we can find ways to counteract all sorts of other pollutants, not just petroleum products. Genetic engineering is just beginning. It's a young science, but we're hoping our progress will be fast. It needs to be fast."

After class that day, Colin Hendrick asked me to stay a minute. He wanted me to help him organize the data from his old high school project about the oil spill and invited me over to his father's house on Saturday. Usually on Saturdays after our soccer game (which is first thing in the morning), Dad has some project for us to do, but I didn't even think about that. I just told him I would.

On the walk home after school, as soon as Evan and Zach and Colby had split off at Market Street and Matthew and I were alone, he started right in again about how genetic engineering was messing with what only God should do. I kept thinking that God didn't make oil spills and fertilizer runoff, and maybe since people made those things, it was people who ought to fix them. But mostly I didn't say anything.

I didn't tell him why I'd been asked to stay after science class. I didn't tell him about being Colin Hendrick's field assistant. I could tell he was dying to know how Colin Hendrick had known my name, and why he didn't confuse the two of us. But he didn't want me to know that, so he wasn't about to ask.

Thank you, Jesus! I thought. I didn't want to share one single thing about Colin Hendrick with Matthew.

CHAPTER TEN

When I told Dad about Saturday, he said that having the noble lariat offer me a job was an honor I shouldn't pass up. Matthew acted like it was no big deal, but I knew he wasn't any too happy about it. I figured it wouldn't hurt him to be a little jealous of me for a change.

We hardly talked to each other all Saturday morning, but it didn't hurt our playing any. The coach wasn't about to separate us for a game, and we passed the ball back and forth just like always. The twin thing isn't about talking. Matthew scored two goals and I scored one, and we won by two points.

Afterward, I walked to Colin Hendrick's house. Or rather, his father's house. A man in plaid pants, white hair sticking out from under a battered old hat, was pushing an old-fashioned kind of lawn mower—the kind with no motor—around the front yard. If this was Colin Hendrick's father, he sure didn't look sick to me. "He's expecting you," the man called, not stopping what he was doing. "Go on up and ring the bell."

It took awhile for Colin Hendrick to come to the door. Though it was a really warm day for the middle of September, he was wearing a flannel shirt again. His hair looked like he hadn't combed it yet, and there were dark circles under his eyes. He looked like he'd been up all night, and I was afraid it wasn't a good time to do whatever it was he wanted me to help with. But he opened the door for me to come in. The minute he did, Lydia came barreling out and jumped all over me, whining and wagging and making such a fuss that he finally had to tell her to back off and sit so I could get through the door. "She's excited to see you," he said. "You may not have had a dog before, but she's never had a kid, either."

Inside, the house was pretty much an ordinary house—lots bigger and nicer than ours, of course, but nothing that would make you think a really famous or rich person might live there. On one side of the front hall was a living room with a big old flowered couch in front of a wall of bookcases jammed with books from one side to the other, with more stacked on top. On the other side of the hall was a dining room with a fancy chandelier hanging above the table.

"Come on out in the kitchen," he said. "I've dug out all the boxes. The trouble is, I wasn't the most organized person in the world when I was in high school. Now either, for that matter, except now I've got people to organize things for me. What we're going to have to do here is a sort of archaeological dig."

I followed him through the dining room and into a sunny yellow kitchen that had sliding doors out to a deck that overlooked a big yard surrounded by a tall wooden fence. On the deck were a lounge with a fat cushion and a couple of wrought-iron chairs with a table between them. The table was covered with books and file folders; there was an open book upside-down on the top, next to a coffee mug. I figured he'd been out on the deck when I got there, and I wondered why, if he'd come home to be with his sick father, the old man was out mowing the lawn while Colin Hendrick was reading in the sun. I decided Mom was just plain wrong about why he'd come back to Bradyville.

There was a bunch of cardboard boxes, some taped shut, some open, stacked on the kitchen table and on the floor around it. Lydia was still pushing at me and insisting that I pet her. I rubbed her ears and then Colin Hendrick pulled open the sliding door and motioned for her to go outside. She looked up at me as if I might tell her something different, but I just shrugged. "He's the boss." As if she understood what I'd said, she turned and went out. He followed her, picked up the mug off the table outside, and came back in with it.

"Want a cup of cocoa or something?" he asked.

"You may need something to fortify yourself for this endeavor."

"No thanks, Dr. Hendrick," I said.

"In this house, Dr. Hendrick means my father. How about just calling me Colin?"

"Okay"—I had to swallow hard before I could manage it—"Colin."

"So—how'd the soccer game go?"

"We won."

"Congratulations." He gestured at the boxes. "So here's what I want you to do. The boxes that are open are the ones I've already checked. You open the others—there's a knife on the table somewhere—and see what you can find. What you're looking for are spiral notebooks labeled 'Beaver Creek,' a couple of plastic boxes full of specimen bottles, and some files of photographs. Those'll probably be in manila envelopes. If we're lucky, they'll be labeled 'Beaver Creek,' too, but I wouldn't count on it. And don't expect all of it to be together. When I went off to grad school, my parents turned my room into a guest room, so they had me box up just about everything I wasn't taking with me. I just dumped whatever was closest to hand in the nearest box and kept dumping till the box wouldn't hold any more."

He pointed to one of the open boxes. "In there I found my Boy Scout badges, a shoe box full of toy soldiers, a black light from my psychedelic period, the themes I wrote for freshman composition in college, and a microbiology textbook—along with assorted T-shirts and one old basketball sneaker. The other one's likely to be here somewhere." He leaned against the counter, took a drink from his mug, and made a face. He dumped the rest in the sink, rinsed the mug, and filled it with water, which he drank quickly, as if trying to get rid of a bad taste. On the counter next to the sink, there were rows and rows of pill bottles of different sizes. "Go to it, Mark. Just start anywhere you want."

He frowned then and ran a hand through his hair. His eyes had that look again, like they were seeing something else besides what was in front of him—something darker than this sunny room. "Give a holler if you find anything. I have something else to do. I'll be back in a while." And then he left, going through a door on the other side of the room and closing it behind him.

I stood there for a minute looking at the boxes and feeling sort of embarrassed. It seemed nosy to be snooping in Colin Hendrick's things, especially with him not even there. But then I glanced over at Lydia, who was lying out on the deck with her nose pressed up against the glass door. She was watching every move I made, and somehow that made me feel a little better. I wasn't *really* alone with his stuff. I found the knife on the table and cut the tape on the nearest box.

I didn't find anything labeled "Beaver Creek" in the first three boxes, but I did find the other basketball shoe. Some of the other things I found really surprised me. I wouldn't have thought a Nobel Prize–winning scientist could ever have been just a regular kid. But he'd had Superman comic books. And a whole bunch of *Mad* magazines. There were lots of science books, too, like I'd expect, and some thin books of poetry. There were spiral notebooks with school notes, but most of them had more doodles than actual notes.

It didn't take me long to get over feeling like a snoop, and then it was fun to imagine what Colin Hendrick had been like when he was a kid. I wondered why he'd saved the things he had—like an empty M&M's bag and a tin Band-Aid box full of pop-bottle caps. On the inside cover of one of the spiral notebooks was a girl's name—Sandra—written over and over and surrounded by doodles, including a bunch of hearts, some with jagged lines through them.

At the bottom of the third box I found a poster that had been rolled carefully but then crushed by everything that had been packed on top of it. There were still dried-out pieces of old tape on the corners, from when it had been hanging on a wall someplace. It couldn't have been anything about Beaver Creek, but I unrolled it just to see what it was—a marijuana leaf. With peace symbols drawn all around it in Magic Marker. I figured he'd probably had it hanging in his dorm room at college. I couldn't imagine daring to hang a poster like that at home, but maybe his parents weren't like my mom and dad.

"I never inhaled."

His voice startled me. I hadn't heard him come in. "What?"

His hair had been combed and he looked a little better than when he'd left. "I never inhaled. Isn't that the answer people from my generation give people from yours when they ask about pot?"

"I never thought—I mean—I—I—" I could feel myself blushing.

"Never mind. I keep forgetting you're a P.K. But even preacher's kids must know about drugs these days."

I shrugged. "Not firsthand."

"Any luck? Any Beaver Creek stuff turn up yet?"

"Not yet." I held up the basketball shoe. "But I found this."

He took it, dug the other one out of the box on the table, and looked at them side by side. "My basketball career lasted half of one season. I wore these out hiking, not playing." He stepped on the pedal that opened the lid of a trash can by the counter and dropped them in. "I can't imagine what I saved them for. Or most of the rest of this stuff, either. What I ought to do is rent a Dumpster and toss it all. Onward!"

He pulled out a kitchen chair, sat down, and cut open another box. It was more fun to look with him there. It took more time with two of us than it had taken with just me looking, because every time I held up something I'd found, he had a story about it. A lot of them funny. After a while, I got the nerve to ask about Sandra. "Ah, Sandra," he said. "The impossible dream. She was a cheerleader and I was a nerd. But she was something! Red hair, green eyes, long legs. And other attributes." He closed his eyes. "Even now I can picture her in her uniform. Amazing what memory can do."

"Does she still live in Bradyville?" I asked.

He shrugged. "If she does, I don't want to know. Thirty years can't have improved her any."

We talked about girls for a while after that, and I found myself telling him about Sophie Salten, who's pretty much of a tomboy, but the kind of girl I'd like to date if I ever get to be the sort of guy girls want to date. Colin Hendrick was the first person I'd ever told about Sophie. I wasn't even sure I'd let myself know how I felt about her before then.

I was the one who found the first of the things we were looking for—a big brown envelope full of photographs. It wasn't labeled, but the top photo was of an oil-coated creek bank. I showed it to him.

"Score one for the field assistant," he said.

His father came in a few minutes later and Colin introduced us. The old man wiped the sweat from his face with a paper towel and got a pitcher of iced tea from the refrigerator. "Has my socially inept genius of a son offered you anything to drink?"

"Cocoa," I said.

"Too warm for cocoa. Want some iced tea?"

"No thanks. I'm okay."

"It'll be time for lunch soon," Dr. Hendrick said, squeezing a lemon into his glass of tea. "What shall I fix?"

"I'm not hungry," Colin said.

"I didn't ask if you were hungry. I asked what I should fix." There was an edge to his voice, as if they were having an argument instead of just talking about lunch.

The two men looked at each other for a moment, and it seemed to me the argument was going on without any words. Finally, Colin shrugged. "Soup, maybe."

"Tomato soup and cheese sandwiches, then." The old man turned to me. "That okay with you?"

"I ought to be going home—," I started, but Colin interrupted me.

"What kind of an assistant are you? Just because you found one batch of pictures doesn't mean you get to skip out before the job is done. It's time for a break, though." He put both hands against his spine and leaned back in his chair as if what he'd been doing had given him a backache. Then he leaned forward, his elbows on his knees, and sighed. I noticed I was a little stiff from leaning over the boxes, too. And now that lunch had been mentioned, I was hungry.

The kitchen table was covered with stuff, so we ate in the dining room. Dr. Hendrick asked me a whole bunch of questions about my family, just to keep a conversation going, I thought. Because Colin suddenly wasn't talking. He just sat there, moving his spoon around in his soup bowl and occasionally raising it to his mouth to take a sip. He ignored the half a sandwich Dr. Hendrick had brought him. In between answering questions, I ate everything in sight. I didn't want the old man to think nobody liked what he'd fixed. When he asked me if I'd like some ice cream, I nodded, then saw that even though both of us had been talking and I'd eaten a whole sandwich instead of a half, we were finished and Colin wasn't. He'd eaten only about half his soup and still hadn't touched his sandwich. But he had put down his spoon and he shook his head when his father offered him ice cream.

After lunch we started on the boxes again. I remembered what Matthew had said about scientists not believing in God, and I wanted to ask if he did or not. Dr. Hendrick had said at lunch that he belonged to St. John's Episcopal, but he hadn't said "we." I couldn't figure out how to bring it up. It seemed like a really personal question just to ask out of nowhere, even after the way we'd been talking before lunch. And Colin wasn't talking any more now than he had at lunch. Dr. Hendrick had put on some classical music in the living room, and it was the only sound except for the crickets outside. When I held up the broken blade of a hockey stick, instead of telling me the story behind it, Colin took it from me and tossed it into the trash, on top of the basketball shoes. "Not worth hanging on to" was all he said.

I didn't know what had changed, but something had. It wasn't long before I found the plastic boxes. Then Colin found the spiral notebooks. "Now what?" I asked. "Do we have everything you were looking for?"

"I think so," he said, and leaned forward again, his elbows on his knees.

"You want me to put all these boxes somewhere for you?" I asked, thinking that as tired as he looked, he probably didn't want to do it himself.

He thought about that for a minute, then rubbed his face with both hands and sat up straight. "That would be good. They go back to the shelves in the furnace room downstairs. While you do that, I've got some phone calls to make."

So for the next fifteen minutes I lugged boxes, two at a time when I could manage it, down the basement steps and stacked them on dusty metal shelves in the dim furnace room. When I had picked up the last of the boxes to take it down, Dr. Hendrick came and stood in the kitchen, looking as if he wanted to say something to me. But when I stood for a minute, waiting, he didn't say anything after all, just turned and looked out at the deck, where Lydia had given up on being let back inside and was lying under the lounge, out of the sun.

When I came back upstairs, turning the light off

and closing the basement door behind me, he held out a glass. "Have a Coke," he said. I took it gratefully, wiping sweat out of my eyes with my shirt-sleeve. "And thanks for helping. All those boxes. All those stairs."

"No problem," I told him, and swallowed most of the glass of Coke in a couple of big slugs. "If I wasn't doing this, I'd just be washing storm windows with my dad and brothers."

"You help around the house a lot?" he asked.

"We all do," I said, and finished the Coke. "Dad does a couple of extra jobs, and Mom does, too, so everybody's expected to pitch in."

"Large families are a good thing," the old man said, taking my empty glass and putting it in the sink. "A good thing."

Colin came in then, his face shut up like a fist. "Randy's screwed up again," he said to his father. "I don't see how they're going to get along . . ." He glanced at me and didn't finish, as if he didn't want to say whatever he'd meant to say in front of me.

"I guess I'll be going now," I said, "if you don't have anything else—"

Colin started to shake his head, and then he looked out toward the deck. "Unless you'd like to take Lydia to the park for her walk—throw a rock for her awhile."

Like to? I thought. Of course I'd like to! "You mean by myself? Aren't you coming?"

He looked over at his father, who was rinsing out

my glass. “I have some things I need to do. I’d really appreciate it. She won’t get her walk today if she has to wait for me to take her.”

“Well, *sure*!” I said.

He smiled then, and his father did, too. It was the first time either one of them had smiled since Dr. Hendrick came in from mowing the yard.

“I’ll get her lead and the two of you can be on your way.” As if she’d heard us, Lydia was back at the sliding door, her nose pressed to the glass, her tail circling. “Just don’t let her get overtired.”

“I won’t,” I promised. “I won’t!”

CHAPTER ELEVEN

At dinner that night everybody wanted to know what it was like working with the noble lariat. I just said it was fine. Johnna wanted to know what kind of a house he lived in, and she was disappointed to find out that it wasn't some kind of mansion. "Everybody says geniuses are weird," Matthew said. "I bet he's weird."

"He's not weird!" I said. "He's nice. Very nice. And funny!" A person could be a little moody, I thought, without people thinking he's weird.

After the dishes were done, Dad went into the dining room to practice his sermon and Luke and Mom and Johnna set up a game of Clue on the kitchen table. I said I didn't want to play and went up to our room, and Matthew came up right after. He came in, fussed around at the desk for a while, taking stuff out of the drawers, putting it back, rearranging the books that were on it, as if he was trying to give himself an excuse for being there. I got my book out and pretended to be reading it, ignoring him. Finally, he cleared his throat really loud and I looked up at him. "What?"

"You want to hear the sermon I'm going to give when Dad lets me do the prayer service again? I've been working on it ever since I got home this afternoon."

What I wanted was to have the room to myself for a while, but I didn't say that. I didn't say anything, and he took my silence to mean—as it always would have before—that I did want to hear it.

"It's about science. I'm going to use the Book of Job, starting with chapter eleven, verse seven. 'Canst thou by searching find out God?' It's all there, Mark. Right there in the Bible. I'll say how science can be a good thing, when it helps us to know more about the world so we can take better care of it. But we can't expect science to teach us *everything,* because the universe is God's creation and we can't ever completely understand it. Only God can do that."

He picked up a spiral notebook from the desk and started flipping through it. "It's kind of hard to understand in the King James Version, so I'm using Dad's paraphrased Bible. The best stuff is in chapter twenty-eight. It talks about the things men can do, like digging mines to find gold and jewels. Digging into mountains and damming up rivers. Growing crops on the top of the earth even though there's fire way down underneath."

He found the page he was looking for. "Here, listen. 'But though men can do all these things, they don't know where to find wisdom and understanding.' Then it goes on to tell all the things God can do. Like making the winds blow and putting the oceans in place. Making the patterns of the rain and the path of the lightning. It says that while people are searching and searching for wisdom and understanding, God knows where those things are all along, and he tells us. God says that wisdom is to fear the Lord and that understanding is to forsake evil. Then I'm going to end with chapter forty-one, verse thirty-four. 'He is a king over all the children of pride.'"

"You want to preach a sermon that says the stuff Colin Hendrick is doing is wrong?" I said. "Genetic engineering and all that?"

Matthew nodded. "Don't you see? The Bible says Dad's right. I'm right. I'll say that even though it *seems* like a good idea to do something that will clean up oil spills, it's not really, because that's messing with the way life works, the stuff humans can never really understand. Scientists who think they should do that are 'children of pride.'"

I found my hands clenched into fists, my fingernails biting into my palms. Just because he'd discovered something in the Bible that seemed to take his side didn't mean he had won the argument. "What about the mess we've made of the world? Go back to all that stuff in Job about what human beings can do. When the Bible was written, they didn't know how big a mess we could make doing that kind of stuff. Mining and damming up rivers and all the things—worse things—they never could have guessed back then that we would be able to do someday. But we do know now. We're supposed to *take care* of the earth. But there are bad things like oil spills that happen to the earth because of us. Things that are *our* fault. We have to do something about them!"

"Yeah, well, there have to be other ways we could clean up oil spills. Ways that wouldn't mean messing around with DNA and changing the basic stuff of life. Scientists ought to be figuring out how to keep oil spills from happening in the first place."

I didn't want to argue anymore. I had a headache. Sometimes we couldn't tell whose headache it really was, because when one of us got a headache, the other one usually did, too. *We* have a headache—that's what I used to think—and a lot of times if one of us took something for it, both of us got better. But this time I could tell by looking at him that Matthew didn't have any headache. He was so caught up in the argument and the idea of giving a sermon to prove his side that he didn't care how much it bothered me. I needed to change the subject.

"I'm quitting the soccer team," I heard myself saying, and could hardly believe it. Where had that come from?

"What do you mean?" Matthew said, and his face lost that triumphant look it had had since he'd started talking about his sermon. "Permanently? You can't do that!"

"Why can't I?" It was as if somebody else had taken over my mouth and was saying things I didn't mean. Except that I knew, suddenly, that I did mean them. That morning, the old twin thing had worked. Where I kicked the ball, there Matthew always was, waiting for it. And when he kicked it, there I was. Neither of us had to think about it. I wasn't even sure we could stop it happening if we wanted to. I'd gone into the game feeling all disconnected from him, and it had happened anyway. "I'm quitting," I said again. "I'll tell Coach MacMahon on Monday."

Matthew's face was a picture of confusion. "But why? I don't understand. We *love* soccer. And we're great at it!"

"Listen to yourself. *We* love soccer. Well, maybe I want to do something that only *I* love. Maybe I want to have something that is mine. Nobody else's. Just mine."

Matthew looked at me as if I'd gone completely crazy.

"Haven't you ever wanted that?" I asked him.

"I have that already," he said. "I have a twin!"

I got up and walked out of our room then, slamming the door behind me.

CHAPTER TWELVE

You'd have thought I had quit school instead of just a soccer team. "But you *love* soccer!" everybody said. Why did my family think they knew the inside of me better than I did? When I didn't back down, Dad said, "Are you *sure*?" looking at me in that minister's way he has that makes you feel like he's looking *through* you and seeing stuff you don't know is even there. Was I sure? I hadn't even meant to do it. But still, deep down I knew the answer. "Yes. I'm sure."

So when Colin Hendrick called to say he hadn't realized what a job teaching eighth-grade science would be and asked if I could come and work with him after school every day, I said yes.

The first thing we did was organize the stuff from his high school project to take to class. Then he had me get some more water from the pond at the park so we could make what he called an "animalcule habitat." All that meant was that we poured it into a great big glass salad bowl. He said it had been his mother's favorite salad bowl till he'd taken it over in junior high to use exactly this way. "My mother would put up with anything as long as I told her it was furthering science." When we set the salad bowl down on white paper and put a bright light right over it, we could use a heavy-duty magnifying glass to watch what went on inside.

Once we did that, I spent a whole lot of time watching the animalcules instead of doing anything that might be called helping Colin. It was as interesting as a television program. Maybe more so, because it was real. He'd sent me to get the new batch of pond water from the shallow, reedy end of the pond with a really big wide-mouthed jar so I could get lots of water and algae, and lots of the muck from the bottom, too. Along with all this stuff came three creatures that were bigger than any of the other animalcules. You could see them perfectly well with your naked eye, and under the magnifying glass you could see them really, really well. Colin said they were the larvae of a water beetle, and they're called water tigers or pond dragons, because they're such ferocious predators. They look sort of like short, pudgy little worms with bristles along their sides and a pair of huge horns on their heads. Only they aren't really horns at all. They're jaws. These guys hang upside down on the surface of the water, with a little tube sticking up like a snorkel so they can breathe, and then snap their jaws shut on whatever creature happens to swim too close. Or they can swim down and hunt for a while in the bottom muck.

The first time I saw one of them catch something in its jaws, it was a water flea. But the water flea was a little too big for it and managed to get loose. I was cheering on the water flea for escaping, but it didn't swim away. It just floated down against the sloped side of the bowl, looking half-dead, till it caught on a little clump of algae. After a while it started moving, but a whole lot slower than usual. It was a really long time before it could swim properly again. Colin said that was because the pond dragon's jaws inject a digestive juice into its prey. That water flea was really lucky. If it had been held any longer, it probably would have died after it got away. If the pond dragon holds on to its prey long enough, it practically digests the creature before it sucks up the juices.

There were three of these pond dragons that first day. A few days later there were only two. And a day after that I saw that the bigger one had caught the other one around the middle and was hanging on, even though the other one was squirming like crazy trying to get free. "Cannibals, they are," Colin explained. "They'll eat anything they can get their jaws around, even tadpoles and small fish." When I was getting ready to go home that day, the one that had been caught wasn't squirming anymore. It looked sort of like an empty sock hanging from the other one's jaws. And by the next day I couldn't find any sign of it anywhere. "Other creatures are probably eating whatever was left," Colin said. "Lots of these animalcules live off dead plant and animal matter. It's a very efficient system."

"Like recycling."

"Just like it. You didn't think *humans* invented recycling, did you? The pond dragon quits being a pond dragon and goes back to being carbon atoms and nitrogen atoms—all the basic building blocks. And those get used to make something new. The process that builds living things up from the first cell gets reversed, and then it starts over. Same thing happens to us, you know. It's the way the universe works. A complex and wonderful system."

"Doesn't sound so wonderful for the pond dragon."

Colin laughed. "Once it gets past the dying part, it's not half-bad."

In the bowl, there were lots of teeny little worms that used the algae (which looked like green hair) and the other junk in the water to make themselves little cocoonlike things on the side of the bowl. I'd be sitting there, watching the rotifers and water fleas rushing around above the bottom muck, and suddenly a long snaky arm-looking thing would come out from a clump of green and sweep around and disappear again. I could never see what it was after—probably some of the microscopic creatures I knew were in there even though I couldn't see them—but it always startled me. Until they came out to grab something, they were really well camouflaged.

The teeny transparent worms that floated around and then suddenly went into crazy spasms of wiggling always startled me, too. That wiggling could take them clear across the bowl in no time, like swimming the length of a pool in a few seconds.

I guess one of the things I liked best about watching all this was that if I put down the magnifying glass and moved a couple of feet away from the bowl, all I could see was greenish brown water with some dark gunk in the bottom. And I knew that even what I was seeing when I was up close and using the glass wasn't all that was going on in there. Probably most of the living things in that little world I couldn't see at all without a microscope. There was something amazing about all that drama going on among creatures so small that most people didn't even know they were there—even though I'd gotten them right there in the pond in the middle of a busy park in the middle of town! It made me think hard about the idea of God being aware of every sparrow that fell. Was he aware of every water flea? Every amoeba? Every pond dragon?

Colin gave me some books so that I could find out more about some of the creatures I was watching. He said it took a real specialist to be able to identify them all, so he wasn't even going to try. But he wanted me to learn as much as I could, as much as

I wanted to, and then I could share what I learned with the rest of the class. We were going to take the animalcule habitat to school so that everybody could watch. It turned out that all the time I spent watching, I really was helping Colin after all. I could tell the kids about it and Colin wouldn't have to.

We gathered a bunch of collecting supplies for the field trips Colin was planning. Buckets and nets and bottom scrapers and glass and plastic jars of different sizes. And we went over maps of Ohio's water systems to see where we might go other than Beaver Creek, which would be our first trip. One day when I got to his house, he had big pieces of green and red poster board spread out across the kitchen table and packs of colored markers. He wanted me to make huge diagrams of the web of life and the freshwater food chain, based on the ones in a college biology textbook. "I want to give your class a real sense of the complexities of the planet's living systems, to make them see where they fit in. I hope to make them care. I'm going to have them write reports on what we find, so you'll need to leave a lot of room on the diagrams to mount their reports."

That was the day he decided I wasn't his field assistant, since we weren't out in the field. "You're more like an apprentice," he said. "And that makes me the master. Biology master, I suppose."

"So, do I call you master?"

He laughed. "Let's stick with Colin."

That was also the day I asked him if he believed

in God. He was standing at the door to the deck, looking out at the yard and talking about how complex the web of life is. "And the best thing about it," he said, "is that we get to be part of it. We get to study it, try to understand it, appreciate it. We're the only part of the system that can do that."

"What about God?" I asked.

He didn't answer for a moment. Then he turned around and looked at me. I set down the marker I'd been using. His answer was more important to me than I'd thought when I asked.

He sighed. "I suppose you mean that father figure up there in heaven, watching over everybody and everything?"

I nodded.

"Well, first, I'm a scientist, and I don't know where this heaven could be. With the newest telescopes, we've seen almost all the way back to the big bang, and in all that immense space, all that immense *time,* we've seen no sign of it. And second, if there's a father-god somewhere taking personal requests, how does he decide whose to grant? Let's say he's looking down on a hurricane coming up the coast and the people in one city beg him to let it miss them. If he deflects the storm a little, it'll hit the next city. But the people in the next city are praying just as hard, don't you think? How would a father who loves *all* of them decide?"

I hadn't ever thought of it that way. I didn't have an answer. "So you don't believe in God?"

He shook his head. "I didn't say that. It's just that my god is more like the force that shaped the universe."

"Just created the universe and went away?"

Colin frowned. "Where would he go? No. I think he *is* the universe. Or the energy that makes it, that runs it. And he isn't a he. Or a she. To me, god, if you can call it god, is a force or a field. Whatever is in and behind and through all of it."

After that, I wasn't about to bring up Jesus.

A lot of what he had me do over the next couple of weeks I did pretty much by myself, because he was busy with other things. He'd go off for long times, and I figured he was keeping in touch with his lab back in upstate New York, where the genetic engineering was going on. His father would come and go, but he mostly stayed in the living room, reading and listening to classical music or opera, or he worked in the yard or the back garden. At some point every day Dr. Hendrick would come into the kitchen and fix me a snack. Crackers and cheese or a cut-up apple or cookies, and always something to drink. Colin just never seemed to think about food. It was no wonder his clothes were so big on him.

Sometimes, after I'd worked awhile or we'd worked awhile together, we'd take Lydia to the park. And sometimes he'd have me take her by myself. When I did that I liked to pretend she was my dog. When people asked questions about her, I'd tell them everything Colin had told me. Everybody was always so impressed with her that I got as proud as if she really were mine.

Everybody in our class knew I was helping Colin, especially after he brought the habitat to school and had me tell them all about the pond dragon and the camouflaged worms. The kids were surprised that Matthew wasn't helping, too. Nobody was used to seeing one of us without the other.

For the first time, I was living a different life from Matthew's. We weren't talking a lot about it. We weren't talking much at all. Mostly he seemed to be avoiding me. Or maybe it was that I was avoiding him. All I knew was that except for at night in our room, we didn't see much of each other.

But that didn't mean I didn't think about him. Or the topic he was going to use when Dad let him preach again. One day while we were watching Lydia dive for rocks at the park, I mentioned to Colin that some people thought genetic engineering was a bad thing—that it wasn't something human beings ought to do. I didn't say it was my family who thought that.

He just shrugged. "That argument's been used by somebody against almost every step of scientific progress," he said. "Human beings ought not to fly. Or they ought not to transplant organs. Never mind how many lives can be saved by transplants."

"But isn't this different?" I asked. "Aren't you creating life?"

"Don't exaggerate what we can do," he said.

"Nobody's anywhere near *creating life.* Tinkering with it a little, that's all we're doing. And human beings have been doing exactly that for thousands of years." He pointed to Lydia as she bounded up the bank with her rock in her mouth. "She's an example of genetic engineering. Ever since we began domesticating animals, we've been in the genetic-engineering business. We breed them for whatever traits we want—color, size, temperament. We do it with plants, too. Corn, rice, beans, you name it. It's all different now from what it was when it grew in the wild. The only thing that's changed is the level at which we can tinker."

I tried that argument out at the dinner table that night, but nobody bought it. They all thought messing with DNA was different. Johnna wanted to know if wild spinach tasted any better than the spinach we were having for dinner. Mom said she was sure wild spinach tasted way worse. "I vote for the noble lariat, then," Johnna said, "if he could engineer spinach to taste like macaroni and cheese."

CHAPTER THIRTEEN

The next day, we had our first field trip, to the place on Beaver Creek where the oil spill happened. Colin had told everybody how to dress for the trip—jeans or shorts (if they knew how to avoid poison ivy) and old sneakers they wouldn't mind getting wet. It was a hot, sunny day, just the sort we'd been having most of September. Everybody else went in the school bus, but I rode with Colin because he had asked me to come over during lunch break to help him load all the collecting equipment into his car.

Matthew made a big show of not minding. But he minded.

The oil tanker had gone off the main highway on a curve and down an embankment. We got to the place from a county road so the bus didn't have to park on the highway and we didn't have to climb a long way down to the water. Beaver Creek wasn't very big here, split by sandbars, with a few sort of deep places, but only about twenty feet across.

Colin hadn't come to check it out first, so he was seeing it for the first time along with the rest of us. When we got to the water's edge, he just stood, shaking his head. There wasn't any sign of the old spill, of course. But somebody had used that curve in the highway as a place to pull off and dump their trash. The tanker truck had knocked down trees as it went, so there was a strip from the top to the bottom that didn't have any of the big old trees that lined the road everywhere else, only shrubs and saplings. All down the embankment there were fat green or black plastic bags, garbage spilling out from holes where some animal had torn through the plastic, or where the bags had just disintegrated in the weather.

There were bottles and cans, stuff that could have been recycled if anyone had wanted to bother, and there was real garbage, too—eggshells and grapefruit rinds, corn husks and coffee grounds, stuff that takes a long time to rot. There were layers and layers, as if people had been dumping here almost the whole time since the oil spill. It wasn't just garbage. There was an old dishwasher, puffy yellow insulation peeling off its sides and top. There was a broken toilet Brady Connor started cracking jokes about the minute he saw it. And half a bicycle. And there were shreds of plastic everywhere, bits of faded grocery bags caught on bushes and even up in the high branches of trees.

"Gross!" Evan said when he stumbled over a bag that spilled out dirty disposable diapers.

Colin didn't say anything. He sat down heavily on the wide silver trunk of a tree that had fallen toward the river from the bank, its top branches in the water. It had been there so long that all its leaves and most of its smaller branches were gone. But trash, floating downstream from the dump place, had collected in the branches that were left, as if the tree were a strainer.

Brady Connor whistled. "You'd have to engineer some big bacteria to eat all this stuff." He poked around the edges of the mess with a stick. "Big and hungry, too. What are we supposed to be looking for?"

"Anything you can find that looks like it *belongs* here," Colin said. "Anything alive." Zach and Sophie had helped bring the collecting equipment over from the car, and Colin explained how to use it. He told us the kinds of animals we were likely to see and the best way to catch what we found—minnows and crayfish and turtles and frogs, snails and slugs.

"Eeeuuuw!" Nicole Burbeck interrupted when he got that far. "I hate slugs."

"In that case," Colin told her, "you can be in charge of finding snakes."

She was halfway back to the bus before the word was completely out of his mouth, and Mrs. Gerston sent Todd Rathburn after her to bring her back. Everybody was laughing when she came back, including Colin, so she got it that it had been a joke, but that didn't help her much. A minute later Colin said that there actually might be snakes around—"harmless ones, as scared of you as you are of them." She didn't believe that part, but she believed that there were snakes lurking—anywhere and everywhere. She totally refused to look under or behind anything or turn over any rocks. She said she would only collect things she could actually see right out in front of her, so Colin gave her one of the butterfly nets and told her to catch flying things.

Colin stayed where he'd settled, on that tree trunk, and anyone who found something would take it over to him. Emery Lewis turned over a big rock and caught a crayfish right away, and Colin had him put it in a bucket with some water and the rock it had been hiding under. Most of the time when someone brought something to him, Colin would call everybody else over to be sure we'd all seen it. Then he'd ask questions about it.

It wasn't like a test, like he expected people to know the answers because we'd studied this stuff somewhere—he said he just wanted people to share what they knew, if they happened to know anything. Then he'd tell us whatever else he thought we ought to know and he'd answer questions. In the car on the way, he'd told me that what he most wanted the kids to learn from this trip was how many different kinds of life there are out there and how they interact with one another and depend on one another. And how in the long run they all depend on the creek.

Emery guessed his crayfish was a predator,

because of its claws, and Colin explained that it ate some kinds of plants as well as fish and frogs. "And what eats crayfish?" he asked.

"People," Sophie said. She has relatives in Louisiana, and she said they eat crayfish a lot. I couldn't imagine eating anything that looked like that, or finding enough meat on it to be worth it, for that matter.

"Raccoons," Todd said. "And herons. And muskrats."

Nearly everybody was surprised when Colin said that fish and frogs eat them, too, sometimes.

Colin talked about the food chain and then asked me to tell what happens when toxic chemicals get into it. He'd told me a lot about that while we were sorting his old Beaver Creek stuff, so I knew enough to do it. Matthew wandered away while I was talking, pretending to be looking for creatures. I was pretty sure he just didn't want to hang around to listen to me playing teacher.

I explained that when a toxic chemical—like dioxin—gets into one creature, the problem tends to go straight up the food chain. A chemical that doesn't actually kill a small animal gets eaten (along with the animal) by the next creatures up the food chain and then those creatures get eaten by the next, and so on. By the time the chemical reaches the top of the food chain, it's likely to have gotten more and more concentrated and more and more deadly. Since people are basically the top of the food chain, toxic chemicals in the wilderness don't only harm the wilderness. They can directly harm us, too. Like when somebody catches fish in a polluted river and cooks and eats them.

When I finished, Colin nodded, and I realized that what I'd just done wasn't all that different from giving the sermon at the prayer service. Only this didn't make me nervous at all.

Asking us questions about the creatures we showed him also gave Colin a chance to find out what people "knew" that wasn't true. Like when Evan brought a garter snake, mostly to scare Nicole with. Brady said some snakes can catch their tails in their mouths and roll down hills like hoops. Colin said that was a folktale, and he gave some other examples of folktales about animals, like porcupines throwing their quills.

Sophie, who isn't the least bit afraid of snakes or anything else, gave Colin a big dripping scoopful of bottom muck she'd gotten from a shallow pool, and he poured it into a white pan and then called everybody around to show them what he said was one of the most awesome predators in the whole creek system. It wasn't much to look at and it wasn't very big, but he said it was mostly mouth. Like the pond dragon, it eats anything and everything it can catch. When he said it was a dragonfly, the kids didn't believe him at first, because it didn't look like one at all. It had no wings and had been living underwater. But it was the larva stage—called a nymph—and he said we should be very happy there are lots of dragonflies and damselflies, because both in the baby stage and as adults, they eat tons and tons of mosquitoes. The nymph, living underwater, eats mosquito larvae and the adult catches flying mosquitoes right out of the air. He showed us some mosquito larvae in the same scoopful of water. He didn't have to show anybody mosquitoes, of course—by that time, most of us had some new bites. He said it had been so warm this fall that there were more mosquitoes than usual for the end of September, and more of a lot of other mostly summer creatures, too.

Todd Rathburn asked what eats dragonfly nymphs. "It's just like with crayfish," Colin said. "The same things that are its prey when they're young and small are its predators when they're bigger." Brady said nature is nothing but a gigantic cafeteria.

Somebody caught a couple of the water bugs that one of the kids called Jesus bugs. Matthew grumped about calling them that—he said it was taking the name of the Lord in vain—but the name made sense. Another name for it is water strider, because it really does walk on water. It eats insects that fall onto the water, and sometimes mosquito larvae, too.

"You'd think with all those predators eating the babies," Brady Connor said, scratching a mosquito bite on his neck, "there wouldn't be so many that live to grow up and drive us nuts."

"That's the way the web of life works," Colin

said. "There are millions of eggs and larvae, so that even with a world full of predators who need to eat, enough can survive to grow up and lay eggs and make new ones."

"I don't think it's very nice for the babies that get eaten," Sophie said.

"That's because you're a person and people care about death. If an egg lives long enough to hatch but then gets eaten as a larva, the creature isn't traumatized about how short its life turned out to be. It just lives till it dies. It doesn't sit around worrying about when and how it's going to die."

"Yeah, well, it doesn't fight back, either," Emery Lewis said. "People would fight back, that's for sure! I would."

"Some creatures do," Colin answered, "and plants, too. They don't all just wait there in the cafeteria line to be snapped up."

"So what do they do?"

"There's a beetle that stands on its head and shoots a chemical irritant at its attacker. Some plants make thorns and spines; others develop natural insecticides. It's all a sort of dance. If you're prey, you evolve ways to avoid being eaten, and if you're predator, you evolve ways to get past the weapons and defenses. It's a challenge to eat and a challenge to avoid being eaten."

"Who eats us?" Todd asked.

"Nobody!" Emery Lewis said. "We're at the top of the chain—didn't you hear? We the Man!"

"Grizzly bears," somebody said.

"Sharks," somebody else put in.

"Mosquitoes!" Brady said.

"We may be the most successful predator on earth," Colin said. "But we're part of the web like everything else. There are plenty of predators after us. We have to scramble like crazy to find defenses against some of them. A lot of the time, we lose."

"To what?" Emery asked. "What can't we shoot or bomb or poison?"

"It isn't just bigger things eating smaller ones. The biggest threat to *us* comes from the smallest things," Colin said. "Microbes. Bacteria and viruses. As fast as we find defenses—medicines to kill them, vaccines to keep them from killing us—they evolve right around them. We think we're pretty tough, with our guns and our bombs and our poisons." Colin paused for a moment, then ran a hand through his hair. "Clever as we are, we're not as in control as we imagine."

"You mean when I get a virus, it's *eating* me?" Emery asked.

Brady made hand gestures like snapping jaws at Emery. "Gobble, gobble, gobble."

"Not quite the way you eat a hot dog. But a virus consumes energy from your body to support its life and reproduction, so it's pretty much the same thing."

"Eeeeuw," Nicole said.

"It's a complex system," Colin said. "An amazing and elegant system—"

"Yeah," Evan said, "if you dig death!"

Colin turned to Zach then, who had brought over a net he'd been swishing around in the water forever, trying to catch minnows that swam away faster than he swished. He'd finally succeeded in catching a couple. So then we talked about fish for a while. Fish eggs get eaten a lot, too, and baby fish, but Colin didn't talk much about that. He probably thought we'd had enough about death. I was thinking it was a good thing only people had souls. Otherwise, heaven would be jammed full of bugs.

We spent a couple of hours at the creek and found lots and lots of living things, not counting plants, which just about everybody considered too boring to bother with. We didn't keep everything we collected. Colin said there was no sense disturbing the natural world any more than we had to. Mostly what we kept to take back to the classroom were creatures there were plenty of. The smaller an animal, it seemed, the more of them there were. We didn't even *see* most of the bigger animals that live in and around the creek (except for birds and chipmunks and squirrels). No raccoons or otters, no skunks or porcupines or muskrats. Colin said we made way too much noise for any of those to come near.

We got back just before the school day ended.

When the other kids went home, I stayed to help Colin and Mrs. Gerston set up an aquarium for the crayfish and some minnows and snails and beetles we'd brought back. Colin mostly sat, leaning forward the way he so often did, his elbows on his knees, while we filled the aquarium with river water we'd brought back in buckets. He gave advice on arranging the rocks and setting up the filter system and then he helped put the creatures in. When it was done, we all sat for a while, admiring how natural it looked. Finally, Colin looked at his watch and started to stand up. As he did, he made a sound that was a cross between a groan and a yelp. He grabbed for the back of the chair, his face going a sort of gray color, and then sat back down.

Mrs. Gerston went over to him. "You okay?"

He nodded. But you didn't have to be a genius to see that the nod was a lie. He clenched his hands on his knees and leaned down so that his chin was almost on his hands.

"Shall I call someone?" Mrs. Gerston asked.

"No," he said, his voice strained. "It'll pass."

"You overdid today," she said. "I'm sorry. I should never have asked you to do this."

For a long time, he didn't answer. He just stayed there, his breath coming in ragged gasps. Something was terribly, terribly wrong. And both of them knew what it was.

"You think this would be any easier if I was just sitting around Dad's house?" he said at last, and there was anger in his voice as well as pain.

Mrs. Gerson shook her head. “I don’t know. Maybe.”

“Nothing makes it easier,” he said.

Nobody said anything then for a few minutes. It felt like hours. I watched the minnows swimming in the aquarium, a snail crawling up the glass. Finally Colin sat up. His face had a little more color in it, but his eyes were still squinted against pain. “I’m sorry, Mark,” he said. “I’d hoped I wouldn’t have to tell you.” He looked at Mrs. Gerston and she nodded.

“I’m sick,” he said then. “Very sick.”

CHAPTER FOURTEEN

Colin Hendrick had pancreatic cancer. I'd never even heard of the pancreas, but he told me what it is. It's important. It isn't something you can just take out when it goes bad, like an appendix. Besides that, it's in a place that's hard to get to. Hard to see even with all the high-tech equipment hospitals have now. And when you get cancer there, you don't get a lot of symptoms. Not till the cancer has gotten really big and really dangerous, and sometimes not till it has spread to lots of other organs, too. That's what had happened to Colin. He'd been so busy doing his work that when he didn't feel so good, he didn't take time to see a doctor. He thought what was wrong with him was indigestion. By the time it really started to hurt, "it was too late," he said, "to do anything. No surgery, no radiation, no chemo—no nothing."

"Does that mean . . ."

I didn't even have to finish the question I hadn't

wanted to ask. He nodded. "I'm going to die. There's nothing anybody can do about it."

When he said that, I felt as if he'd poured ice water down my throat. Cold moved down my chest and into my stomach and then just spread through my whole body. I felt like I was turning to ice from the inside out.

Little things get us, he'd said. Bacteria. Viruses. He hadn't mentioned cancer cells. All of a sudden I understood a lot of things. His clothes being too big for him, his father pushing him to eat. Why he sent me to the park with Lydia by myself so often.

Lydia. It seemed terrible to think about Lydia when I'd just found out Colin was dying. But Lydia was only ten. It wasn't Colin who would lose his dog this time. It was his dog who would lose him. I thought of how she watched him, how she seemed to understand everything he said. As hard as it is for a person to lose a dog, at least the person understands. Lydia wouldn't understand. He would just be gone one day. My throat seemed to close up and I couldn't swallow.

"How long?" I asked.

"Nobody knows," he said. He looked at Mrs. Gerston then. "Not as long as I thought, it seems."

He said he was going home to rest, asked me if I wanted to take Lydia for her walk. I told him no. Maybe tomorrow. The truth was I didn't want to see Lydia. Didn't want to think about who was going to lose who. I especially didn't want people to think she was mine. She wasn't mine. She was his. The reason he had to go home at night.

He offered to drop me at my house, but I shook my head. I wanted to walk. I wanted time by myself before I had to see Matthew or Luke or Johnna. Before I had to pretend the world was still okay. Colin didn't want people to know about his illness yet, but he said I could tell my family, if I asked them not to tell anyone else. I didn't want to tell them. I didn't want to talk about it. I wasn't sure I could.

When we were leaving, going through the big front door that Colin was holding open for us, Mrs. Gerston patted my shoulder. I twisted away from her hand. I didn't want to be touched. It was all I could do to be standing. Walking. Moving ahead through the air that felt as if it was pushing back at me.

On the way home I remembered what Colin had told Emery about prey animals defending themselves, fighting back. And I got mad. Colin wasn't defending himself even, let alone fighting back. He had just given up. "There's nothing anybody can do about it," he'd said. How did he know that for sure? He was a scientist. *He'd* found a way to solve a problem nobody thought could be solved. There had to be a scientist somewhere working to solve this problem, too. Why wasn't he finding that scientist? Even helping him? Besides, people survived cancer. It happened all the time. Why couldn't it happen to him?

Why did he just say he was going to die? Why did he say "nothing anybody can do"?

I picked up a stone and threw it as hard as I could at a maple tree whose leaves on one side were just beginning to turn color—red and orange streaking the green. The stone crashed through the leaves and landed in someone's yard. I hated the colors suddenly. They meant that the leaves were dying. I kept my eyes low then, on shrubs and bushes, anything that was still green. And saw something I'd never noticed before. Almost every single leaf of almost every single bush had holes. Chewed edges. Something—some little things, insects or caterpillars or whatever, had been eating them. All of them. There was hardly a leaf anywhere that was whole. "An amazing and elegant system," Colin had called the food chain. Suddenly I agreed with Evan. If you dig death.

Colin Hendrick was going to die. Soon. That fact had settled into my head like a splinter of glass that I couldn't get rid of. A splinter that kept working itself deeper.

I walked very slowly. I didn't want to get home. I couldn't imagine how I could go into the house and pretend to be my normal self. And if I didn't, somebody would want to know what was wrong. Somebody would ask and I would have to answer. Maybe I could have gotten away with it if it was just Mom and Dad and Johnna and Luke. But Matthew would be there. No matter what had been happening to us the last couple of weeks, we were still twins. Matthew would know. For all I knew he already did. For all I knew he had felt the ice water in the center of himself as soon as I'd felt it.

Finally our house appeared in front of me, its white paint peeling, its porch sagging a little, Dad's rusty old blue Buick in the drive. Next to the house was the concrete block building with the cross on the roof, the Rock of Ages Community Church, its big old sign in front. On the sign, along with Dad's name and the times of Sunday and Wednesday services, it said STAND ON GOD'S PROMISES. THEY DO NOT CHANGE.

I stopped still and read it again. Dad changed the slogans the first of every month, and I'd seen this one every day for nearly four weeks, but I felt as if I'd just read it for the first time. God's promises. "Ask, and it shall be given you."

How could I have forgotten that? As soon as I remembered those words, another memory came with it—a sermon Dad had given a long time ago about some doctors who had done studies that proved—proved!—prayer could heal. Maybe Colin Hendrick thought there was nothing anyone could do. But Colin was only a scientist. Nobel Prize or no Nobel Prize, he didn't know what we knew. He didn't know about God's promises.

Thank you, God, I thought, and then, Thank you, Jesus! I hurried toward the house. Everything had changed. Now I couldn't wait to tell my family.

Because I needed their help. I needed every one of them to pray for Colin. Starting tonight. Starting right now. There was something to do all right, and the Filkins family would do it!

CHAPTER FIFTEEN

I told them at dinner, and Mom's eyes filled with tears. She reached over to pat my hand, and it was all I could do not to pull it away. I still didn't want anybody to touch me! Right away, Johnna started asking questions, some I could answer and some I couldn't. She wanted to know what *pancreatic* meant. She wanted to know how Colin Hendrick got sick.

Mom explained that we really didn't know the answer to that. And we weren't very good at curing some kinds of cancers, either. "Can this kind be cured?" Johnna asked.

Dad said that this particular kind of cancer was especially bad, and then Johnna asked the question that was too hard for me even to think about, the question I'd been avoiding from the minute Colin had told me. "*Why* did the noble lariat get pancreatic cancer?"

It got very quiet then.

"We don't have answers for questions like that," Dad said finally. "This is one of God's mysteries. A tough one."

It was time to ask what *I* needed to ask. But I wasn't sure what Dad would say after all that stuff about genetic engineering being wrong. Did he think the cancer was God's punishment for the work Colin did? Did he think Colin didn't deserve our prayers? There was only one way to find out. "Can we have a family prayer service after dinner to pray for him?"

I hadn't needed to worry. Dad didn't wait. He had everybody put down their forks right then and there.

"Heavenly Father," he said when we'd clasped hands around the table, "we interrupt this bountiful meal to ask that you be mindful of Colin Hendrick in his time of need. We don't know why or how this illness has come to him, but we ask your mercy. May his pain be eased and his spirit set at rest. May health return so that from this time forward he can lead a life filled with fruitful endeavor, using his gifts in your service. Please grant that he may have, as Johnna would expect, a long and *noble* life. We ask it in the name of your only Son, our Savior Jesus Christ, acknowledging that in all things it is thy will, not ours, that will be done."

Then he told everyone to be sure to remember to add Colin Hendrick to their personal prayers that night. "And every night till he gets well," I added. Dad said he would ask both the men's and the women's Bible Societies to pray for him, too, and he'd put his name into the regular services in the place where he prays for the sick. When I said that Colin didn't want anyone to know about his illness yet, he said the public prayers could be anonymous.

"We can pray for *our brother who is gravely ill.* God knows our intentions."

After that, dinner was much quieter than usual. Through the whole thing, Matthew didn't say a word. I knew he was thinking about me and Colin and Colin's illness. The splinter of glass in my mind wasn't quite as painful now, but it was still there. Maybe Matthew was feeling it, too.

It was our turn to do the dishes. I washed and Matthew dried, which was how it usually worked. Sometimes we talked while we worked and sometimes we didn't. That was another part of the twin thing—that we didn't have to talk all the time, any more than you talk to yourself all the time when you're alone. But this time it was different. I could feel Matthew purposely not talking, holding back something he wanted to say. I pretended not to notice. The hot dishwater felt good tonight, maybe because I hadn't ever really gotten warm again after the ice water feeling. As I washed glasses and plates and silverware, I worked out a prayer that I said over and over in my mind: Please, God, let Colin be well. Please don't let him die. Please, Jesus, heal him. Take away his pain.

When we finished the dishes, we watched TV for a little while and then went upstairs and started on our homework. We were sitting in our usual places, me on my bed and Matthew at the desk, when Matthew slammed his notebook shut and turned the chair around so he was facing me.

His mouth was thin and his nose looked all pinched. There was the same kind of sadness in his eyes there was in Mrs. Gerston's when she had patted my shoulder that afternoon. "I have to say this!" he said. "This won't work. It can't."

"What won't?" I knew what he meant. But I wanted the words out in the air where I could argue with them.

"Colin Hendrick hasn't taken Jesus for his personal savior. He doesn't even believe in God."

"He does too!" What did Matthew know about Colin Hendrick? Nothing. Nothing at all. "He just doesn't use the same words."

"Words matter. Names matter. 'He that believeth in me . . . If ye ask it in my name.' If names didn't matter, then what would be the difference between Muslims and Buddhists and us? There wouldn't be any point being a Christian."

"If it won't work, then how come Dad didn't say so? How come he prayed?" I asked.

"Because you asked him to." Matthew's face was pink now. My mirror. Mine probably was, too. "I'm sorry," he said. "I really am! But the Bible says—"

"The Bible says a lot of things!" I wasn't going to talk about it anymore. I turned so that my back was to Matthew, picked up my math book, and pretended to be looking at it. What if Matthew was right? What if to be healed Colin had to be a Christian? Had to *say* he was a Christian. I thought of the words that had repeated themselves in my head that time Colin and I were talking about God—that if he didn't believe in Jesus, he would go to hell. Together, those two ideas were like bombs going off one after the other. He couldn't be healed if he didn't believe, and if he couldn't be healed, he'd die. Then, when he died, he'd go to hell. Forever and ever.

Tears blurred my eyes. I rubbed them away, but more just kept coming. It wasn't any good being mad at Matthew. He was just saying what we'd learned all our lives. "I am the way, and the truth, and the life. No man cometh unto the Father but by me." This was right at the center of what we believed. How could I get around it?

Colin *had* to be healed. If he got healed, there would be time for him to change, time for him to find the way and the truth and the life. *Help me, Jesus!* I thought. *Help me!* It wasn't like a prayer. It was more like a scream inside my head.

Then I remembered a picture from the children's Bible Matthew and I had learned to read from. A picture of Jesus in his long white robe, his brown hair hanging down to his shoulders, holding his hands out to a man with deformed legs crumpled under him, who was sitting on the ground at Jesus' feet. They were surrounded by a crowd of people. On the facing page there was another picture of the same man, standing on two perfectly good legs, his hands in Jesus' hands, both of them smiling, and the people around them shouting and laughing and hugging each other. I had always loved those two pictures. They were proof of the miracles Jesus could do. Jesus had made the blind see and the lame walk. If Jesus could do that, he could take away pancreatic cancer. Even after it had spread. And Jesus didn't ask people before he healed them if they believed in him. He just saw they were sick and he healed them. He did it because he loved people and didn't want to see them in pain. So why wouldn't he do that for Colin, no matter what Colin believed? Why couldn't he? Why wouldn't he?

Then, as if I'd been struck by lightning, I remembered something else. I put down my math book. Matthew had opened his notebook again, but he wasn't looking at it.

"John, chapter fourteen, verse twelve," I said. "'He that believeth in me, *the works that I do shall he do also; and greater works than these shall he do.'* And verse fourteen, 'If ye shall ask anything in my name, I will do it.' Colin doesn't have to believe. *We* have to believe. And we do! That's all that matters. We can heal him!"

Matthew looked at me. He didn't say anything, and I wasn't even sure he *wanted* Colin to get healed.

"It's a promise! That's why Dad had us pray. It *can* work! It has to." We sat there staring at each other, eye-to-eye, mirror-to-mirror. "This is important, Matthew. The most important thing in all my life. Can you be with me in it?"

Matthew thought about it for a while. I'm not sure either one of us breathed the whole time. Finally, he nodded.

"Do you remember Dad's sermon about the doctors proving that prayer helps?" I asked.

"Sure."

"The more people there were praying for somebody, the better the prayers worked. I have to get everybody praying that I can. Not just the Bible Societies. Our church is too small."

Matthew nodded again. I could see the old Matthew come back into his eyes. "I know what we can do." He went out into the hall and got the telephone book from the table by the upstairs phone. He opened it to the Yellow Pages and found the heading "Churches." "We'll split the list up and we'll call every church in town and ask them to put him on their prayer lists. Everybody has to have a prayer list."

It was Matthew taking over again. Matthew deciding what the two of us would do. And I didn't care.

We each made a phone list. It was too late to start calling then, but Matthew promised to start on his right after school the next day. It wasn't a soccer day. By the time I got home from Colin's, he could be finished and I could have the phone to do mine.

When Luke came up, we said our bedtime

prayers, and I prayed for Colin, mostly saying what I could remember of what Dad had said at dinner. Then, in the silent part, I repeated what I'd made up doing the dishes, over and over again. Please, God, let Colin be well. Please don't let him die. Please, Jesus, heal him. Take away his pain.

Later, as I pulled up my covers and tried to settle myself for sleep, I looked up at the depression Matthew's body made in the mattress over my head. If Matthew was in my bed and I was in his, he would be seeing the exact same thing.

Matthew and I could do more for Colin than I could do by myself, I knew. There was more to each of us when we were together. Like we were multiplied. Twins were all about math. We were one egg added to one sperm and then divided. Now we would be multiplied, working together, praying together. Me times Matthew, I thought. Matthew times me. Then I realized that couldn't be right. Because one times one was still only one. To be *more* than one, we needed to be added, not multiplied. And to be added, we needed to be separate. Different. One Mark plus one Matthew.

One Mark and one Matthew would do this. We would work a miracle. We would save Colin Hendrick. And then there would be time for him to find Jesus *and* he would be able to go on helping to save the planet. That wasn't just *my* will, was it? It had to be God's will, too!

I pictured the sign in front of the church as I felt

myself drifting off to sleep. Colin Hendrick was leaning against it, smiling. Lydia, her tail wagging, stood with him. Stand on God's promises, I thought. They do not change.

CHAPTER SIXTEEN

I woke up early, to a day that was gray and drizzling rain, and began saying my prayer over and over in my head. I got dressed and in and out of the bathroom, still repeating the prayer, before Luke and Matthew were even up. Dad was at the table when I got down to the kitchen. "You're up early," he said.

I stopped repeating my prayer long enough to answer. "You too."

"I have to talk to somebody at the welfare office this morning, and I want to be the first one in the building."

I asked him to tell me more about the scientific studies on prayer, and everything he said made me feel even better. It turned out that the person who was prayed for didn't have to believe for the prayers to work. Even though I really did have faith that what we were doing would work, I was glad to know that. It was as if science and religion were agreeing for a change.

All day at school, whenever I didn't absolutely have to be thinking about something else, I repeated my prayer, over and over, over and over. My Uncle T.T., who's an evangelist down in Texas, talks a lot about the need to bring prayer back into public schools. He would have been surprised to know how much prayer happened at John Glenn Junior High that day. It wasn't only me, either. At lunch Matthew and I went into a corner of the cafeteria and had a little prayer service. He'd rounded up Evan Elsasser and Denise Currier, who both go to St. John's Episcopal, and got them to pray with us. We didn't tell them who they were to pray for, just told them there was a person we knew who was very sick and might die and needed prayers. Denise thought this was a great idea, but I had the feeling that Evan only agreed to pray with us because Denise did—they're going together. I told him nobody would have to know what we were doing. Evan hasn't ever seemed to me to be a very religious sort of person.

Denise said she'd get Father Gilman, their minister—rector, she called him—to add this person to his prayer list for Sunday. St. John's was on my list, so that was one phone call I wouldn't have to make. But she wanted to know the person's first name. She said Father Gilman always prayed for "Mary, your servant," or "John, your beloved child," and she wasn't sure it would work if we didn't have a name.

Colin's first name was too unusual to tell her. The secret would be out right away if we did that. "There are about a gazillion Marys and Johns in the world," I told her. "If God can figure out which one your minister's talking about when he prays, he can figure out who we mean without having that person's first name. Just say it's one of God's children who is very sick."

"Is it a kid?" Evan asked. "Do we know him?"

"It isn't a kid," Matthew said. Once Evan knew we weren't talking about a kid who might be going to die, he didn't even notice that his second question hadn't been answered.

When school was over the rain had stopped. It was still gray and had gotten chilly, but I could see some spots of blue between the clouds, which seemed to mean it might clear up eventually. I practically ran all the way to Colin's house, splashing right through the middle of puddles in the sidewalk. I didn't care if my feet got wet. I just wanted to get there and tell Colin the good news. I got into a rhythm of saying my prayer in time with my footsteps. *Please, God, let Colin be well. Please don't let him die. Please, Jesus, heal him. Take away his pain.* I knew the words so well now, I figured I could say them in my sleep.

I'd decided just to tell Colin about the scientific studies that showed prayer helped to heal people. No sense telling him that it might be an extra good thing if he had faith. Unbelievers, Dad always says, either don't listen or can't hear, which is what makes missionary work so hard. It isn't that they don't have beliefs; it's that they have different ones, and it's hard to get around them. If Colin wasn't ready to trade his belief in the force that created the universe for a belief that Jesus was the way and the truth and the life, that was okay. But since Colin was a scientist, I was pretty sure he believed in scientific studies.

When I got there, I rang the doorbell and stood, sort of hopping from foot to foot, saying my prayer in my head, till Dr. Hendrick came to the door. Lydia burst through when he opened it and jumped all over me as usual. "I'm sorry, Mark," Dr. Hendrick said, "but Colin isn't feeling well. No working today. He asked me to ask if you'd just take Lydia to the park."

"Can I come in and see him?" I asked. I just *had* to tell him the news!

But Dr. Hendrick shook his head. "He's sleeping," he said, "and I don't want to disturb him. He doesn't sleep that well at night."

I guessed Colin had told his father that I knew about the cancer. This was the first time he'd admitted that Colin wasn't feeling well. Before, when Colin had wanted me to take Lydia to the park by myself, there had always been some excuse about his needing to do some work or make some phone calls or something. I was disappointed, but I wouldn't have wanted to wake him up for anything. "Maybe he'll be up by the time we get back," I said.

"Maybe," his father said, and held the door open. "You know where her leash is."

I got Lydia's leash, and we went to the park. The first part of the way, she frisked all around me and I kept having to change hands with the leash to keep from getting tied up. She liked me. I knew she did. Dogs, or Lydia at least, don't play games. They can't talk, but that doesn't mean they can't communicate. If they like you, they let you know it. Lydia hadn't ever had a kid, Colin had said. Now she did. I wondered if that would help her if Colin— And then I remembered that he wasn't going to die. He wasn't!

"You don't have to worry about that," I told her. "You aren't going to be all alone in the world after all." She cocked her head, the way she nearly always did when someone talked to her, as if by tipping her ears she could understand English better. "He's going to be okay. The Filkins family is on the case!" After that, I went back to saying my prayer. Since I had Lydia with me, I said it out loud. I know God can hear our deepest thoughts, but it always seems better to pray out loud, just in case he isn't listening hard enough. Or he's tuned in to somebody else's deepest thoughts. People wouldn't think I was crazy if they noticed I was talking; they'd just think I was talking to Lydia.

I had her rock in my backpack. We played with it for about half an hour. And then I told her she'd had enough and put the rock away. Finally she gave up begging me to change my mind and went off to sniff around the bushes along the shore, where all those ordinary dogs spend their time. I was just sitting on the bench, thinking the prayer and watching her, when shafts of sunlight suddenly came down between the clouds—honey golden rays that looked like beams straight from heaven. "Glories," Mom calls those beams. No wonder people said the streets of heaven were paved with gold. You could just imagine angels going up and down those beams like big golden escalators, white robes, wings, halos and all. I went back to repeating my prayer again, thinking the glories might be a sign from God that he was listening. I must have been concentrating hard, because I didn't hear him behind me until I felt a hand on my shoulder. I nearly jumped out of my skin.

"Sorry. I didn't mean to startle you." Colin came around the end of the bench and sat down. "She all finished diving?" he asked.

I nodded. He was wearing a rain jacket zipped up over his flannel shirt. In the orangey light of the glories, his face looked better. Less haggard. I wondered if our prayers were working already. "Your father said you were sleeping."

"I was. It was a minor miracle. I lay down around noon, and the next thing I knew, it was four. That may be the longest uninterrupted sleep I've had since I got here."

It *is* working, I thought. *Thank you, Jesus!*

"I thought a little fresh air would do me some good." Lydia, from halfway around the end of the pond, had seen him and came bounding back.

Without slowing down, she leapt straight onto the bench between us and licked his face, her tail circling, her body quivering with joy. The way Lydia greeted someone she liked, every single time it looked as if she'd given the person up for dead and was rejoicing at his resurrection. He put an arm around her and patted her for a moment before he made her get down. She frisked around his legs then, demanding a game. "Mark snitched on you," he told her. "I know you've already had your workout." He leaned down and picked up a stick. "You can play a little old-fashioned fetch, though." He tossed it away and she went after it, but you could see with every step she took that she was just doing it to humor him.

"Will you look at that sky!" he said. And then he sighed. "Sometimes I wish the world would restrain itself a little."

He tossed the stick a few more times, and Lydia dutifully chased it and brought it back, her coat almost dry now. I told him about the prayers, about the studies that showed they worked. He listened, but he didn't seem as excited as he should have.

"It's working already," I said.

"You think that's why I had my nap?" he asked. His smile gave him away. He didn't believe it.

"But you said it was the longest sleep you'd had since you came here! We started praying for you last night, and today you slept."

"Beware of assuming that just because something

follows something else it was caused by that something else. It's an old trap we rationalists have to beware of."

"But the studies *proved* prayer works," I told him.

He shook his head. "Mark, there are studies and there are studies. Some good, some bad. I'd have to read them for myself to decide which these were. And even the good ones don't *prove* anything; they just suggest interpretations of observed events."

"But . . ."

He patted my arm. "Don't get me wrong. I'd be the last person in the world to tell you to stop. If the sky is going to put on displays like this, I'd like to hang around a little longer to watch. Just because the studies can't prove prayer works doesn't mean prayer *doesn't* work! I'll take any help I can get." He frowned. "Any that doesn't force me to eat seaweed or get stung by bees or sleep standing on my head."

Which is how I knew how little he had believed me. As if prayer could do no more for him than silly stuff like that. It doesn't matter what he thinks, I told myself. It doesn't matter. The only thing that mattered was *us*. And we'd keep doing it. And I had faith. I knew it would work. "Ask, and it shall be given you."

"Mark, I'm touched that your family would make an effort for me. I just don't want you to get your hopes up. Four hours of sleep without being wakened by pain are a blessing, and however that happened, I'm grateful. But even if it was your prayers, that's a long way from a cure."

A collie, its owner carrying its leash, came along the path and Lydia went up to greet it. They sniffed at each other for a while and then bounded away together.

"Jake!" the man called. The collie ignored him.

"Lydia!" Colin shouted. "Come!"

Lydia swerved in a big circle and came back, the collie following. Lydia sat in front of the bench, looking up at Colin's face, and the man came and got the collie.

"Sorry," Colin said, clipping Lydia's leash to her collar.

The man had leashed the collie now and was pulling him away. The collie was none too happy to go. "Jake!" the man scolded, his voice peeved. Then he spoke to Colin. "It's not your fault. Everybody's dog should obey the way yours does!"

When the man had gone on around the pond, Colin pushed himself up from the bench. I could tell from his face that the effort hurt, but he didn't make a sound. "Let's walk. It's a long time since I considered the possible value of exercise."

"Do you have a middle name?" I asked as we started walking.

He raised his eyebrows at me. "Sure. Taylor. It was my mother's maiden name. Why?"

"Oh, I was just wondering," I said. In case all those ministers, like Father Gilman, insisted on having a name for their prayer lists, I wanted to have a name to give them. This is the Taylor they'll all mean when they pray, I told God. "My middle name is Thomas," I said.

Colin sort of chuckled.

"What's funny?" I asked.

"Wasn't Thomas the doubter?"

"Yeah, but he only doubted till Jesus showed him proof."

"Oh, right," Colin said. "I remember."

CHAPTER SEVENTEEN

It was October now, and Matthew and I had gotten Colin onto the prayer list of every church in Bradyville that had a prayer list. Denise thought it was such a good idea to pray for "Taylor" that she organized a bunch of kids that she knew went to church regularly and even Joel Saperstein, who's Jewish, to pray with us every day during recess. She said prayer was prayer and she didn't think it mattered whether it was Christian prayer or not. I thought of Jesus telling the disciples they could heal in his name and I wondered whether it would work with Joel in the group. But Denise insisted that ecumenical prayer groups were extra strong and extra good.

Sophie's aunt belonged to something called a healing circle, so she asked her aunt how one worked. From then on, Sophie and Denise made us all sit in a circle at the beginning, holding hands and sending light and healing thoughts to "Taylor, who's very sick and maybe dying." After that, which seemed way too weird to me to count as prayer, Matthew led a regular prayer. He did it instead of me partly because he wanted the practice but mostly because something went wrong with me whenever I tried to pray for Colin with other people around. I got choked up and couldn't get any words to come out. It happened once and I didn't try it again, in case I might actually start to cry.

Sophie decided that while we were at it, we ought to pray for more than just one person, because there were probably lots of other people in Bradyville who were sick and maybe even dying, too. Matthew added "anyone else who is sick in Bradyville" to his prayers, and then Sophie wanted him to do anyone who was sick in Ohio and then in America and then in the whole world, but Matthew said that would weaken the effect and he refused to go any bigger than Bradyville. He said anyone who wanted to do the whole world could do it at the beginning, in the healing circle part while they were sending light. "It won't be the healing circle stuff that works," Matthew had told me after the first day.

"Yeah, but they like it, and it gets people to stick around for the prayer part who might not do it otherwise."

We swore everybody who came to the group to secrecy. We were afraid that since prayer wasn't allowed in school we could get in trouble, even though we were only doing it at lunch hour and not in class. Every so often somebody new found out what we were doing and joined us. But mostly everybody kept it quiet and nobody gave us any trouble.

I told Matthew the prayer I was repeating over and over, and he began to do that, too. I didn't think he remembered to do it as often as I did, but at least when he did, that made two of us. One plus one. We both used exactly the same words, in case that would make it stronger.

And as the days went by, it really did seem to be working. Colin's face smoothed out a little, and the circles under his eyes got less noticeable, as if he was sleeping better. He didn't seem to get out of breath so easily. Our sessions at his father's house got longer. Instead of just having me do stuff to help him with what he was teaching the rest of the class, he had begun to really teach me biology. He said he wanted me to understand what it was that had made him choose his life's work. He had me bring in flowers and plants from the backyard when we were doing plants, and he used the color plates in his old textbooks when we were doing animals. Most of the time he just talked, asking me questions, answering mine.

Twice he walked to the park with Lydia and me, and he insisted on being the one to throw her rock for her. It was one of those times when I asked him about heaven.

We were walking back toward his house along a path through a little stand of woods between the pond and the park baseball diamond. Colin put one foot carefully in front of the other and we were moving very slowly. I could hear his breath going in and out through his open mouth. Lydia was sniffing at every tree we passed, as if we were walking so slowly on her account.

"Since we haven't found heaven with telescopes, does that mean you don't think there is any such thing?" I asked him.

"Not after we die," he said.

"But that's the whole point of heaven, isn't it? Where we hope we go after we die?"

"Worried about me, are you?"

"No," I said, wishing it were true. I didn't want to be worried. We weren't going to let him die, and everybody could see he was getting better, so I didn't really have to be worried. Still, I remembered those glories coming through the clouds. Whether we could see heaven with telescopes or not, I knew there had to be such a thing. It was one of the promises. And when I thought about heaven—and Colin—I couldn't help but worry.

We came out of the little woods. There was a bench beside the baseball diamond. "Let's sit," I said. I could hear that he was out of breath, understood suddenly that even if he was better, talking while we walked was hard for him, the way it was hard for Matthew and me to talk on the last of ten laps around the soccer field. Please, God, let Colin be well, I began again.

Lydia looked at us questioningly as we sat, and then she lay down by our feet, her nose on her paws. After a few moments Colin spoke. "What do *you* think heaven is?"

I shrugged. "A place where you can be with God, forever and ever and ever. Mom says it's like going home."

"You already know what I think happens when we die—what I said about recycling. We go back to the stuff we came from. For that, there's scientific proof. 'Ashes to ashes, dust to dust,' so to speak. I know you believe that something more than that happens. That there is something to us other than our bodies. The 'I' of us that goes on."

"The soul," I said.

"Right. Only there's no proof of that, no experiment that can test for this thing that you believe you and I have and Lydia doesn't."

Hearing her name, Lydia raised her head and looked at us. It had never seemed strange to me before that we should have souls and animals shouldn't. But now that I knew Lydia, it did seem strange. Unfair. There was something behind her eyes, I thought, just like there was something behind mine and Matthew's and Colin's. Why shouldn't that something get to go on like we did? Why wouldn't God care about Lydia the way he cared about us?

"I don't see a difference," Colin said. "Lydia's as much an individual as I am. You couldn't mistake her for any other dog, not even another springer. She's a distinct personality. We're both creatures who belong to the web. So why should there be any difference between what will happen to Lydia when she dies and what will happen to me when I do? There's no scientific proof of soul; all we know for sure is what happens to our bodies. When Lydia and I die, we'll disperse. Both of us."

"You think there's no life after death," I said, wondering how he would ever come to accept what Jesus came to tell us. Eternal life was the whole point. The most important message humans had ever been given.

"I didn't say that." He stared at the empty baseball diamond for a while. "Of course there's life after death. It *grows out of* death. Ever since it began on this earth, life has been unstoppable. There's no reason to believe it will end anytime soon." He stopped and I listened to his breath rasping a little even though he was sitting down. A crow called from the woods.

"The thing is, it won't be *my* life that goes on, not as Colin Hendrick. Believe me, I've thought a lot about this in the last few months. When I die, Colin Hendrick will be gone. Nonexistent. Just as I was nonexistent before I was born." Colin shivered and pulled his jacket closer around him.

I didn't want to think about this. The crow called again, and then another and another. Three of them flew low over the field. I concentrated on watching them as they swooped up to land in the treetops.

"There's something wonderful that can happen to us while we're alive. When we feel we're doing what we were somehow always meant to do, being our best selves in the best-possible way. Using everything we are to accomplish something worth doing. Like when Lydia's down at the bottom of the lake, using that remarkable gift of hers, finding that rock. That, it seems to me, is heaven. The moment when we're absolutely successful."

"Like when you got the Nobel Prize?"

Colin shook his head. "Not then. That was a very nice thing, a joyful moment. But it isn't what I'm talking about. For me it was the time, after years of failure, when what I was trying to do actually *worked.* I knew the principle made sense, that it was theoretically possible. But we could not make it work. Time after time the new organisms died. And then one day that changed. They not only survived; they not only consumed oil as we'd hoped they would; they began to reproduce. And their offspring consumed oil, too. We didn't have all the problems solved, but it had worked. Theory had become reality. Everything I am went into that moment."

Colin stopped, leaned forward, and rubbed at Lydia's ears. His face was drawn, and I could tell he was hurting. But there was a brightness to his eyes now, and his smile lit his face around the pain. "I think *that* was heaven, Mark. Whatever created this astonishing universe, this raging miracle of bits and pieces that fit together in infinitely complicated ways, I had found a tiny key to how those bits and pieces work. And it wasn't just that I could understand it. I could use it! I could take a bit from here and move it there, and the result of that moving was a living being that survived and did what we needed it to do. More than that, it grew. More than that, it made copies of itself. If God had really knelt down by a riverbank to mold Adam out of clay, his feelings would have had to be just like mine that day.

"God the creator and man the creator. Working together. In your terms, it was as if I was kneeling on that riverbank right next to God. An apprentice to the Master." He sat up then, winced, and leaned forward again. "That one moment was worth every terrible moment in my whole life. That one experience of heaven wiped out every second, every nanosecond of hell."

I leaned forward, sat the way he was sitting, elbows on my knees. That put me looking down at the ground, where a drowned worm lay, skinny and pale pink, in a puddle under the bench. "And you think that's *all* heaven is?"

"That's all I know of it," he said. I could feel him looking at me. I turned my head and our eyes met. "That moment is what I have to show for my life, Mark. I never married. Always thought there would be time for that later. I don't have children to carry on my genes or my name or my work. But that moment, building something new out of the building blocks—that was what I'd been born for."

"But it's over. It's over and you're—" I stopped. "You're . . . sick."

"What you mean is, I'm dying. Everybody has to eventually. I didn't arrange my life very well, as it turned out. I should have thought about people more than I did. Connected with people. I wish I had." He sighed and reached to pat Lydia again. Her tail began its circular wag. "Still, I can say that I'm lucky. Because no matter what, I know my life had meaning."

"Because you did something for the world?"

"No." He pushed himself to his feet. Lydia got up and shook herself. "Because I experienced heaven and I *know* I did."

"But that's not enough."

"I'm afraid it'll have to do. It's all I'm going to get."

It doesn't have to be all, I thought. I didn't say anything, though. And we didn't talk on the way home. Colin was too busy breathing and I was too busy praying.

CHAPTER EIGHTEEN

When he came to class on Friday, the ninth of October, Colin sat only part of the time on the stool Mrs. Gerston put out for him. We had already put up the web of life and food chain diagrams I'd made and he'd grouped everybody and assigned their research topics. He asked the groups to make informal reports about what they'd been doing. He talked some more about the animalcule habitat and the mason jar full of pond water I'd brought in to replenish the water in the habitat when it evaporated too much. The pond dragon had grown enough so we could really see the difference, and still there were lots of little animated punctuation marks swimming around in there.

Then he launched into his "life is everywhere" talk. "Complex, amazing, and everywhere."

He had me spread newspaper out on the lab table and empty onto it a bucket of dirt we'd dug from the garden in his backyard. "This dirt happens to be from my father's yard. But imagine instead that it's the top one inch of soil from one square foot of forest floor." He held up a piece of cardboard to show how big a square foot is, then held it an inch above the edge of the desk. "That's it. One inch by twelve inches by twelve inches. Now, if we don't count anything, like bacteria and spores and single-celled animals, that we can't see without a microscope, how many living creatures do you think that pile of dirt from a forest floor would contain?"

There were lots of guesses, from "four" to Brady O'Connor's joking "five hundred and twenty-two." "Nobody has it right," Colin said. Then he had the class vote—"fewer than 4," "4 to 100," "101 to 600," and "more than 600." Most people voted for "4 to 100." People mentioned ants and worms and grubs and spiders. Somebody said moles, but Todd Rathburn said a mole was too big to fit into the top inch of soil. Nobody, not even Brady, voted for "more than 600." Then Colin announced that everybody was wrong. "The average number of living creatures has been found to be more than thirteen hundred."

Nobody would believe him. So he named off what would be there. Mites, springtails, millipedes, beetles, the larvae of a bunch of different insects. "Next time you're walking along what you think is a deserted path in the woods, think about that. You're never, never alone! Wherever you stand, in the inch of ground beneath your feet, you're outnumbered by around a thousand to one. And if you could count the microscopic life-forms, too, you'd be talking about millions and millions."

"Is this just in the woods?" Matthew asked.

Colin shook his head. "It's very nearly everywhere. There are some deserts, some very high places, and some very cold places where the numbers go way down. But even in the desert, there are more life-forms than you'd imagine. We're so used to thinking of living things as being big enough for us to take notice of that we haven't any idea of how surrounded we are by other lives. Or if we know—like I do—we tend to forget."

Nicole said she wanted to forget, or she'd never want to walk outside again. Some of the other kids agreed with her. "As long as they're so little," Emery said, "it's okay by me."

"This brings us to another interesting bit of information," Colin said when the class had settled down again. "You know how to do averaging in math, don't you?" People nodded. "Okay, then, here's a question for you. If you were to measure every single animal on the planet, what would the 'average' body size be? That's every single animal, from the blue whale, which is the biggest mammal on earth, down to the amoeba. You don't have to come up with height and weight, just a general comparison. Like as big as an elephant or as a big as a house cat."

His answer this time was almost as hard to believe as the first. Most people had guessed around the size of a house cat, trying to balance out things like ants against whales and elephants. But Colin drew a tiny little circle on the board and filled it in with chalk—it was more like a dot—no bigger than a housefly. "Remember," he said when people protested, "that the smaller things are, the more of them there are."

Then he asked who believed in miracles. Lots of people, but not everybody, raised their hands. "Who makes miracles?" he asked then.

Some kids said God; some others, including me and Matthew, said Jesus.

"And how often do they happen?"

"Practically never," Matthew said. "That's why they're called miracles. If they happened all the time, they'd just be ordinary life."

Colin nodded. "Okay." Then he pointed out the classroom window at the big old sycamore tree that grows between the front of the school building and the sidewalk. "That's a sycamore tree. But we don't have to be that specific. We can just call it a tree. Any old tree. Is a tree unusual?" We all shook our heads. "A miracle?" Everybody else shook their heads again, but I didn't. I knew Colin well enough to know that he was laying another trap. "It's losing its leaves now, but it still has plenty. Where did they come from? And what makes them?"

"The tree makes them," Todd said.

"Out of what?" Colin asked, and when Todd just shrugged, he answered it himself. "Out of minerals and water and sunlight, apparently. The tree's roots supply the minerals and the water. You ever think about how much of the tree you can see and how much of it you can't? Trust me. There's more tree underground than there is above. The water, with the minerals dissolved in it, goes up the trunk to the very top, out every single branch and every single twig. It can go up that tree at a rate of a hundred and fifty feet an hour. Last summer, that tree probably moved a ton of water in a single day. And it made more than a million leaves, which used their billions and billions of green cells—chloroplasts—to make food for the tree. How do they do that?"

Nobody answered.

"Exactly. No scientist on earth knows how those cells do that. Now, I don't know what you all think, but to me, that tree is a miracle. It's a whole lot of miracles." He paused for a minute and looked around the classroom, looking at each kid in turn.

"There are miracles as amazing—" He stopped. "No—*more* amazing than that going on right this minute inside every single person sitting here in this room. You listen to me with ears that collect sound waves out of the air and send them to a brain for processing. That brain contains as many cells—millions of them—as the Milky Way galaxy has stars."

"Maybe Todd's does," Brady Connor said. "But not mine."

Colin nodded at him. "Even yours, Brady. Of

course, there's some question about what you do with them!"

"Not much," Zach said. Brady threw a pencil at him.

"That brain in each of your skulls processes the sound waves your ears collect and makes sense of what I'm saying in ways that nobody—*nobody*—understands. We've gotten so we can describe some of the processes in the brain, but don't let anybody fool you. We don't really understand them. Miracles. We are surrounded on all sides by miracles, every single minute of every single day. It's just that we've gotten so used to them, we take them so for granted, that we don't even notice them." He looked at Matthew. "We call them ordinary life. What I want you all to see is that there is no such thing as 'ordinary life.' Every bit of it is miracle. For a very long time," he said then, "I'd forgotten that. But it's the reason I became a scientist in the first place. To see what I could learn about the miracles. The ordinary miracles."

During the time Colin was talking, almost nobody even moved. It was like he had the whole class hypnotized.

If I'd stood up right in the middle of it and told everybody that Colin Hendrick was the Taylor some of them had been praying for, the one who was so sick that he was maybe dying, nobody would have believed me. I wouldn't have believed me. It was as if energy was flowing out of him to everybody in the room, like a tree sending water from its roots to the teeniest branches. Thank you, God, I thought, as he gathered up his stuff and told us he'd be back on Monday. I looked over at Matthew, and he nodded. Thank you, God, we were both saying.

The next morning our phone rang at 8:30. It was Dr. Hendricks. Colin had been taken to the hospital.

CHAPTER NINETEEN

Dr. Hendrick had called 911 in the middle of the night because Colin was in pain, more pain than he'd ever had before, and because he couldn't breathe. He had been admitted to the hospital and was getting medication for the pain and oxygen to help him breathe.

"But he was getting better!" I said into the phone, wanting to yell it. Wanting to tell Dr. Hendrick he was wrong. It wasn't possible. Not after yesterday. Colin had talked for more than an hour and never once had to stop to catch his breath. He'd been getting better. The prayers had been working!

Dr. Hendrick's voice sounded tired, faded. It cracked and rasped, but it was also matter-of-fact, as if he was talking about a car that had been taken to a garage with a blown engine. "There are ups and downs with cancer, Mark. But the tumors are growing. His lungs are fully involved now. You shouldn't kid yourself. The cancer is spreading faster than anyone expected. The best we can hope for is to buy a little time."

"How much time?"

There was a long silence at the other end of the phone. Then: "Weeks. If we're lucky."

Lucky. *Lucky!* Our prayers had been working. I knew they had. What Dr. Hendrick was saying was impossible. If I could just see Colin, I could tell him that the doctors had it wrong. His father—everybody—had it wrong. "I want to see him. Can I go see him?"

Dr. Hendrick told me I couldn't. The only kids under fourteen allowed to visit patients were family members. I put down the phone. Matthew, half-dressed, was standing next to me, his soccer socks in one hand. He knew what Dr. Hendrick had said. I could see it in his face. "It'll be okay," he said. "We'll pray some more, that's all."

And suddenly, I wanted to slug him. I wanted to smash my fist into that face that was my face, that mouth that was saying what my own mind was telling me. What I wanted to hear: "We'll pray some more, that's all." That's all! I had heard it in Dr. Hendrick's voice. That was not enough!

Mom had come upstairs into the hall where the phone was. "I'm sorry, Mark," she said, and put her arms around me, patted my back. "It's hard." For an instant I pressed my face against her, wanting her to hold me and make things all right, the way she could do when I was little and had scraped my knee. But then I felt like Colin, unable to get my breath. As if I was being smothered.

I broke away from her and ran downstairs, ran outside in my pajamas and bare feet, and across the driveway to the church. I went inside, down the center aisle and up to the altar. Above it hung the big wooden cross Dad had salvaged from a church that was being turned into a private school. I knelt there on the step in front of the altar. "You promised!" I said. "'Ask, and it shall be given you. . . . Knock, and it shall be opened unto you.' Well, I've been asking and asking! 'Please, God, let Colin be well. Please don't let him die. Please, Jesus, heal him. Take away his pain.' Couldn't you hear me? Should I have been saying it louder?" I yelled then as loud as I could. *"Please, God, let Colin be well. Please don't let him die. Please, Jesus, heal him. Take away his pain!"* My voice seemed to come back at me from the walls, bouncing back as if it couldn't get up and out where it could be heard. Where God was hiding. Or where he wasn't listening. Didn't care. Maybe, after all, he'd just created the system, set it running, everything eating everything else. Death everywhere. And then turned his back.

"You promised!" I said. I'd been kneeling, and now I sat back on my heels. "I believed in you, just like you said I had to. I've always believed in you. 'When two or more are gathered together in my name, there will I be also.' We gathered in your name. Not just Matthew and me. Not just two.

More. Lots more! And we all prayed. We did everything you said. But you didn't take away his pain. You let it get worse! You didn't heal him. You let him get sicker!"

I heard the door open behind me. The light from outside fell across the altar and the base of the cross and then went away again as the door closed. Dad came to the front of the church and knelt beside me. "Our Father, who art in heaven," he began, "Hallowed be thy Name. Thy kingdom come. Thy will be done—" He stopped. And then he repeated the last phrase. "Thy will be done, On earth as it is in heaven."

When he went on, I joined him, saying the rest of the words with him, as I had done more times than I could remember. And when we had both said "Amen," he turned to me. "The hardest time is when his will is not the same as ours."

"He promised," I said. "'Ask, and it shall be given you.'"

"And it *is* given. Always. It's just that sometimes it's a long time before we understand what it is that he gave us. No matter what it looks like, it's always a gift."

I looked up at the cross. It was two pieces of wood, hanging from a wire. I don't believe you, I thought. I don't believe you anymore. But I didn't say it.

I got up and walked out. He didn't follow me. Matthew and Luke and Mom and Johnna were all in the kitchen when I went inside. Nobody said anything as I went through and upstairs. In our room I lay down on my bed, staring up at the underside of Matthew's mattress. Miracles. Colin found them everywhere. But where were they when he needed one?

I stayed there all morning. I could hear Mom and Dad talking downstairs, Luke and Johnna and Matthew going out, coming in again. But they all left me alone. I don't know if I went to sleep or not, but I don't think so. Some of the time, in spite of myself, I repeated the prayer again. I'd been doing it whenever there was nothing else to do for so long, my mind just did it all by itself, running it around and around like when a tune gets stuck in your mind. The difference now was that I didn't believe anymore that it could help. Whenever I noticed I was doing it, I did my best to stop.

It was after noon when the phone rang, and it was for me. It was Mrs. Gerston, calling from the hospital. Her voice was almost cheerful. "It pays to be a Nobel laureate," she said. "Colin has told the people at the hospital that if all it takes to get you in to visit him is a biological relationship, he'll genetically engineer you to fit their rules. So they've relented. I can come pick you up in half an hour, if you want to come."

If I wanted to come? "I'll be ready," I said.

Colin had a private room. But in a hospital all that means is that yours is the only bed. It doesn't mean things are any nicer. The walls of the room were painted beige and the tile floor was beige, too. There was a television set hanging from the ceiling on a big swivel arm and there was a fluorescent light fixture in the ceiling and another on the wall above the head of his bed. There were two plastic-covered chairs and a food tray on wheels. There was also a bedside stand with three drawers and a telephone and a big vase of flowers. And there was a picture on the wall across from the bed. It was a painting of hollyhocks growing along a fence.

Colin's bed was cranked up so that he was sitting and there were two big pillows behind his back. Instead of a plaid flannel shirt, he was wearing a white gown with little round purple designs all over it. His legs were covered by the white bedspread, but you could see how thin they were—like two jointed sticks. His face looked kind of yellowish and there was a plastic thing clipped into his nose with clear plastic tubes that went up over his ears and around to meet under his chin, where they joined like a Y into a single tube. That tube ran across his chest and attached to a silver spigot that stuck out of the wall. One of those metal IV stands held a plastic bag with what looked like water in it, with a tube coming down from the bottom. Beneath the bag was a blue metal box that also had a tube coming from it. Those two joined and looped down and then up again to an IV that was held into the back of Colin's hand by two wide bands of adhesive tape. On his other hand there was a little plastic thing on his first finger that glowed red. It was attached by a wire to a machine behind the bed that showed numbers, also glowing red, and a thing like a bar graph that pulsed up and down with his heartbeat. He raised his hand and waved the glowing finger at me.

"Pulse-ox," he said. "Monitors the oxygen in my blood."

I nodded. He looked very different here, with tubes and wires running everywhere. Smaller. His neck looked too skinny, and I could see the bone that ran from shoulder to shoulder and the little indentation under his Adam's apple. "What's in that?" I pointed at the plastic bag hanging from the rack.

"Dextrose mostly," he said. "The other tube brings the stuff for pain. See the button there? If I need more medication, I just push it." He grinned, then lowered his voice. "They think I don't know that the dosage is preprogrammed. I can push the button as often as I like, but I can't get more than the doctor decrees I should have. Supposedly there's a psychological effect knowing you can push the button whenever you hurt. Placebo effect, it's called." He waved his hand toward the chairs. "Sit!"

I sat in the chair closest to him. "Does it work? Does it stop the pain?"

He sighed. "It helps. It also makes me fuzzy, so I don't push it if I don't have to. I've demanded something better, something I can take home with me so I don't have to hang around here, trussed up like a

Thanksgiving turkey. They're looking into the situation."

I looked at the tubes leading into his nose. "Can you have the oxygen at home, too?"

Colin sighed again. "Yes. But I don't want to use oxygen any more than I have to. I don't want to go to your class with this thing up my nose, dragging a little green oxygen bottle. It would not be cool."

"Cool doesn't matter," I said. "Breathing matters."

He smiled. "Someone has taught you well. That's one of nature's little truths." He looked at me and squinted. "You still praying for me?"

I swallowed. Was it praying if your mind just ran the words over and over again like an advertising jingle? Was it praying if you didn't believe it? "Do you want me to?"

"Can't hurt, right? No unpleasant side effects."

"I thought it was working. I was sure it was."

Colin was picking at the bedspread with two fingers. "No way to know for sure. I *was* better for a while. Maybe it was just an up time. Or maybe the prayers had something to do with it. Whichever it was, it was worth having."

"But are you really getting better?"

His fingers went on worrying the bedspread, but he didn't answer for a long time. I thought maybe he had forgotten the question. He said the pain medication made him fuzzy. Then he said, "No. And I won't. But that doesn't mean I didn't *feel* better for a while. And it doesn't mean I won't feel better again. For a little while, anyway."

"Your father talked about buying time."

He shrugged. "That's the same as buying life, you know. We're all going to die. The question is only when. It's a very important question."

"When can you go home?"

"Soon. They want me to eat more." He pointed to a glass on his tray with a straw sticking out of it. "If you can call it eating. Want a taste?"

"What is it?"

"The label suggests its resemblance to a chocolate shake. See what you think." He took out the straw and set it on the tray, then held the glass out to me. "Go ahead. Take a taste."

I took a tiny sip. If chocolate shakes really tasted like this, nobody would pay for them. I shook my head.

"My opinion exactly," he said. "I've never been able to stand the stuff."

"I could bring you a real shake," I said. "I could bring you whatever you want."

Colin chuckled and shook his head. "That's the trouble. I don't even want the real thing." He took the glass back from me, looked at it for a moment, and then took a long drink, shuddered a little, and set it back down on the tray. "I'll force it down if it'll get me out of here sooner. You'll walk Lydia later?"

I nodded. "Anytime."

"Good. And I have another request. I want you to

take my place in your science class on Monday. I'll make sure you know what you need to know."

"I don't know if I can. . . ."

"Of course you can. If they ask questions you don't know the answer to, you just tell them that. You can ask me later."

"Why me? Why not Mrs. Gerston?"

"Because you're my apprentice. Because you know more about what I'm trying to communicate to the kids than she does right now. And because you care."

Did I? Did I care any more about algae and pond dragons and the web of life?

"Mark—"

I looked up and met the blue intensity of his eyes.

"I was joking about the hospital rules, about genetically engineering you so you could visit me. But in a way I meant it. If I could make you my son, if I could do that somehow without stealing you from your real family—I'd do it."

I looked down at my hands, at the ID bracelet on my wrist. Mark T. Filkins, it said. What would it have been like to grow up with Colin Hendrick instead of with my family? An only child, not a twin. Just me at the center of everything? I couldn't even imagine it. Anyway, if that had been true, I'd be sitting in the room just as I was now, except that I would be about to lose my father. I felt tears filling my eyes. I shook my head. "Having a son wouldn't keep *you* alive."

"Don't get me wrong. I don't mean just to have a son. Just to leave my genes behind, keep the Hendrick family line going, although my father's bothered about that. I mean you. I'd rather have you as my son than my apprentice." He leaned back against his pillows and closed his eyes. "It's selfish, I suppose, but I'd like to know I had really connected with somebody while I was here. Been that kind of important in at least one person's life."

I rubbed the tears away. "You don't have to be a father for that."

Colin opened his eyes again and smiled. He started to lean toward me, and the shadow of pain moved across his face. He fell back against the pillows.

"Push that button for me, would you?" he said. I did. "And have Ginny—Mrs. Gerston—bring you back tomorrow. We'll go over the material for Monday." He closed his eyes, and I started to get up to leave. He opened them again. "Thanks for coming," he said.

"Thanks for making them let me."

Please, God, let Colin be well, I was saying in my head as Mrs. Gerston drove me home. He'd asked me to do it. I'd do it. But I had seen what he looked like in that hospital bed. And I didn't believe in any of it anymore. Not any of it.

CHAPTER TWENTY

And so it began—what I started to think about as the endgame. A terrible waiting game, where there wasn't even any question about who would win, just when. I did the class on Monday, like Colin wanted. I told them about what happened to the web of life and the food chain during the winter. About which things dig down into the mud at the bottom of ponds or streams and which ones, like frogs and toads, find sheltered places on land. About how even when ice forms on the water, enough sunlight gets through to keep photosynthesis going in the algae and water weeds. They listened, at least. And Mrs. Gerston said I'd done a good job. But all the time I was talking about Colin's miracles of adaptation, the ways life handles the ice and the cold of winter, I was thinking that Colin wasn't going to get through the winter. There were no ponds deep enough to let him get beneath the ice, no soft mud to burrow into.

I took Lydia for her walks in the park. That was

the only time when I could forget the waiting for a while. Watching Lydia disappear under the water and come back again, shaking spray from her ears, practically grinning around the rock she held between her teeth, I could be almost happy. Somehow Lydia's happiness, doing that strange thing she did, over and over, just for the fun of it, was catching. The way she pranced around in between, barking, jumping, wagging, so excited that she couldn't hold still till I threw the rock again and she could plunge into the pond after it. Somehow that made things seem right. Until I remembered I had to stop her. Until I remembered that the reason she couldn't just dive for as long as she wanted to was that she was getting older. That she'd be in pain later from overdoing. And someday, not too long from now, she wouldn't be able to do it anymore. And then someday, she'd die.

Colin came home from the hospital on Tuesday. I went to see him after school. And nothing was the way it had been before. There was a hospital bed in the living room now and a big green oxygen tank. And even though Colin was dressed in his regular clothes instead of that awful hospital gown, nothing could hide how thin he was anymore. How his cheekbones and the ridge of his nose stood out in his face. Instead of a big IV stand with a blue machine to deliver pain medication, he wore a little computer thing in a pack on his belt. It had a keyboard to program how fast a syringe attached to it delivered the medication into a tube that ran under his shirt and into his arm at his elbow. As long as he didn't move around too much, he didn't have to have the oxygen tube in his nose. But when he went out anywhere, he did. When he went out, he carried an oxygen bottle that looked like a big thermos over his shoulder.

We'd go for walks sometimes, if the weather was nice enough, but we didn't go far. Even so, he'd point out every little live thing he saw as we moved slowly along. He'd lost his appetite for food, but it seemed to have been replaced with a huge hunger for looking at little live things. Ants. Beetles. Sometimes we'd stop and cut open a leaf gall just to see the eggs or the larva of the fly or the wasp who'd made it. As if to prove there was life inside. And sometimes something else would have gotten there first, some tiny predator. There'd be a pinprick of a hole in the gall and the eggs would be gone, or there would be only dust—dust to dust. Once, when a flock of geese went by overhead, flying south, honking like grumpy drivers in a traffic jam, he stood still and watched them. When they had gone, he still stood looking up at the pale blue sky where they had been. And then we walked on, both of us knowing he would not be here when they flew back.

Mostly he didn't go out, except on the deck, where he would sit on the chaise longue if it was sunny, and he'd watch whatever parts of the web of life he could see in the backyard. He had me bring him the reports the kids were turning in, one section of the assignment at a time. One season of the year or one bit of the food chain. I'd read them to him and he'd tell me what to say to the kids about their work. He refused to grade anything. He said he wanted them to appreciate the planet for its own sake, not because they were getting a grade. "It's the idea of rewards, outside rewards, that destroys everything," he said. "Eventually, you forget everything else." He began to cough then and had to quit talking.

At home everybody was treating me just about the same way Colin was being treated. I expected Luke and Johnna to begin whispering around me, the way people do when a sick person's resting. Everybody was too careful. And that just seemed to make it worse. Everybody prayed for Colin before and then after every meal. I did, too. Because I'd promised. *Some of us keep our promises!* I told God after the "Amen." Wednesday night Dad did the prayer service and preached about God's gifts. I didn't listen. I sang the hymns. I said the Lord's Prayer with everybody else. Matthew and I passed the collection plate. Everything was the same as it used to be. Except that I wasn't there.

Mom made casseroles to take over, casseroles that Dr. Hendrick picked at but Colin never touched. He joked about no mere food being able to compete with his wonderful milk shakes. The stuff he drank came in a whole bunch of flavors, and he made me try every one. As far as I was concerned, one was more terrible than another. But he did his best to drink them. A hospice nurse came and told his father to add ice cream and flavored syrup and mix it all up in a blender. After that Colin drank a little more. Mrs. Gerston brought pints of ice cream in different flavors so he wouldn't get bored. "A doomed effort," Colin said. "The taste of the stuff comes through no matter what! Canned milk and vitamin pills." And then he started coughing again.

At first Colin tried to keep on with my apprenticeship. But he'd get out of breath, or the books he'd want to show me got too heavy for him to lift, or he'd start to cough. So then we'd just sit. Lydia would come lie at our feet, her chin on Colin's shoe. It made him get out of breath to get dressed, but he did it anyway, every day. As if staying in his pajamas was giving in. I'd talk about everything and nothing much. He liked to hear stuff about my family, about when I used to play soccer, about my friends and school. Anything, he said, a father would know, or want to know, about his kid.

Once he told me he wanted to hear what it was like growing up a twin. He said with his interest in genetics, he ought to know more than he did about what it was like for two people to have identical genes. And so I tried to tell him. It was like thinking back to a book I'd read a long time ago. "Twin things" weren't happening anymore. Not since the morning he'd gone into the hospital. Nothing was happening in my life anymore except this waiting game. But he wanted to know about twins, so I did my best. I told him about the times when one of us would be sick and the other would feel the symptoms. About the dreams we dreamed together. And how we didn't always have to talk to have a conversation.

"See?" he said when I was done. "What did I tell you? Science has barely made a beginning. We think that sort of thing ought to be impossible. We don't know *anything* yet!"

That night, during dinner, I watched Matthew eat, listened to him talk about the new strategy Coach MacMahon was trying to get the soccer team to learn before the game on Saturday. And I knew then that he was going through regular life the way I was saying prayers, just to do what people expected him to do. He was playing the waiting game, too. It was the only thing that was real in both of our lives. Except that we were waiting for different things. I was waiting for Colin, and he was waiting for me. As if after Colin was gone, I would come back, the way the geese would come back in the spring. As if everything would be the same again.

Dad had decided to let Matthew preach the sermon at the prayer service the second Wednesday after Colin got out of the hospital. I was glad he hadn't asked me if I wanted to preach, too. If he had, I might have told him the truth. The truth I was hiding, like telling a lie, every time I prayed. Matthew had been planning to preach about not messing with

God's creation. And I knew I couldn't go. I couldn't sit there, listening to Matthew say that what Colin had spent his life doing, the thing that gave him his experience of heaven, was a wrong thing. I was planning to pretend to be sick, till Matthew told me at dinner that he'd changed his mind. He was using a different text. And he'd planned the whole service just for me. So I went. I had to.

I sat next to Luke because we were to take up the collection. Dad began the service as he always did, with the Lord's Prayer. And then he announced the first hymn, number 192, "God Will Take Care of You." I didn't know whether Dad had picked it or Matthew had, but it didn't matter. It was meant for me. "'Be not dismayed, whate'er betide,'" the congregation sang, "'God will take care of you. Beneath His wings of love abide, God will take care of you.'" I moved my mouth, but I didn't sing. God wasn't taking care of *me* by letting Colin die!

Dad did the Scripture readings. I stared up at the cross hanging over the altar. Two pieces of wood on a wire, I thought. And then Matthew was standing at the pulpit. Carolyn Dirkman groaned, but Matthew paid no attention. He wasn't shaking. I could see—I could *feel*—that he wasn't nervous this time. He took a deep breath and began, and I remembered what Colin had told me about talking to the class. What mattered was whether you cared about what you were saying. And Matthew cared. He cared and he wanted me to care, too. I kept my eyes down, focusing on the hymnbook I was holding in my lap. But I could feel his eyes on me as clearly as if they were his hands, and I could hear his words.

"Chapter eleven of the Gospel of John tells the story of Lazarus," Matthew said. "Mary and Martha and their brother Lazarus were friends of Jesus. So when Lazarus got sick, Mary and Martha sent word to Jesus to come and heal him. But Jesus didn't come. He told his disciples that the reason Lazarus was sick wasn't so he would die, but so Jesus could prove something. And Lazarus died. When Jesus finally went to them, Lazarus had been in the tomb for four days, and Mary and Martha were upset because Jesus had always been their friend, but he hadn't come in time to save their brother. Jesus didn't scold them for their lack of faith. He cried with them. But then he told them to take him to the tomb and roll away the stone. When they did, Jesus asked God to let Lazarus live again, and Lazarus, all wrapped up like a mummy, walked out of the tomb.

"Sometimes we ask Jesus to do something we want him to do and he doesn't do it. But it's never too late. He can do more than we could ever believe. Even when it seems there's nothing left to hope for. If he could raise Lazarus from the dead, he can do anything. Jesus told Martha, 'I am the resurrection and the life; he that believeth in me, though he were dead, yet shall he live: And whosoever liveth and believeth in me shall never die.' And then he said, 'Believest thou this?' That's what he's asking all of us. 'Believest thou this?' Are we going to tell him we don't? Could we look our Savior in the eye and tell him we don't believe what he has told us?"

Matthew's voice stopped. I could feel Johnny Schmidt behind me kicking the pew and I heard the sound of his sister smacking his leg to make him stop. Finally, the silence had gone on so long, I thought Matthew must have lost his place, or forgotten what he meant to say next. I looked up, and he was looking at me. "Could we?" he said again.

I'd only preached one time in my life, but I knew that Matthew was breaking a rule about preaching. You talk to the whole congregation, not to one particular person. And you never ask one person a question and expect him to answer it right there in front of everybody. So I didn't answer. I opened the hymnbook and pretended to be looking for something. I paged past "Count Me" and "Truehearted, Wholehearted," and "Carry Your Cross with a Smile" and stopped at "To Eternity."

"Of course we couldn't," Matthew went on finally. I didn't listen to the rest of what he said. I knew perfectly well what it was.

The snake in my stomach was gone now. Something bigger had taken its place. Something bigger than I was. Bigger than Matthew and me together. And it was eating everything in sight. I listened to Dad's prayers, to the one about Colin, using Colin's whole name now that there was no more secret. And then to all the other prayers Dad prayed every week.

The other ones God didn't listen to—about peace and abundance and brotherly love. How could we have listened to those prayers week after week our whole lives and not wondered about it? Not wondered why they never came true. For two thousand years people had been asking in Jesus' name for peace on earth, and we weren't anywhere near it. "Possess your soul in patience," Mom said. Well, my soul was out of patience.

And then everyone was standing and Mom was playing the piano. Luke took the hymnbook from me and opened it to number 95, holding it up for both of us. "'Take the name of Jesus with you, Child of sorrow and of woe,'" everyone sang. "'It will joy and comfort give you, Take it then, where'er you go.'" As they were singing the chorus, I went past Luke and into the aisle. Mom hit the wrong chord and then fumbled for a minute, the voices fumbling, too. I walked past the Schmidts and the Dirkmans, past Elbert Hode and his wife and the Johnsons and Miss Kunkle in the back row, then out the door. Mom had recovered and the chorus was going on. "'Hope of earth and joy of Heav'n'" followed me out into the chilly October air and then faded as the door closed behind me.

CHAPTER TWENTY-ONE

When Matthew came into our room, I was sitting at the desk, staring at a scrape on my knuckle I didn't remember getting. I had known he would come, but not that it would be so soon. I thought he'd wait till the social hour was over, after everybody had told him what a good sermon he'd given.

He closed the door behind him and leaned on it. "You shouldn't have left," he said.

"You're right." I didn't look at him. His face wouldn't be a mirror of mine anymore. Because he had something now that I didn't. Or maybe it was the other way around. Maybe I had something he didn't. "What I should have done was not go in the first place. Leaving was the best I could do."

"It isn't too late," he said. He came and sat on the corner of the desk.

His blue dress pants had lost their crease. So had mine. Maybe those were mine and not his. I should check in the closet, I thought, and see.

"It's never too late. He could get better," he said.

"No. He can't. Everybody knows it." I could hear a car start up by the church, and I wondered who was going home without getting their refreshments. What was the point of Wednesday service if you didn't have the dessert after?

"Even if he doesn't—" Matthew stopped.

I picked at a little flap of skin on my knuckle. It pulled away and a dot of red appeared where it had been. So small it might be just a couple of blood cells. If I were a plant, I thought, the dot would be green. Red blood cells and the chloroplasts in plants were almost the same thing. *I know too much biology. I can't see anything in the world the same way anymore.*

"Even if he doesn't get better," Matthew started again, "he won't die. Not really. The Gospel promises—"

"That if he dies, he'll go to hell. That's what the Gospel promises. He's not a Christian, Matthew! 'He that believeth in me, though he were dead, yet shall he live.' That's supposed to make me feel better? Colin doesn't believe in Jesus. He believes in complexity. He believes in the 'infinite creation of the new.' He believes in the rearrangement of building blocks. Jesus doesn't say anything about that stuff, does he? Matthew and Mark and Luke and John had never heard of red blood cells or chloroplasts or carbon or DNA. So why should Colin listen to them?"

"He could change his mind." There was a whine

in Matthew's voice. Who is he trying to convince, I wondered, me or himself? "Dad says that sometimes, when people are dying—"

"Dad doesn't know Colin!"

"Dad knows God."

"Dad's God would send Colin Hendrick to hell forever and ever because he uses different words than we do! Well, I don't want anything more to do with Dad's God." I stood up so fast, the chair fell over behind me, and I pushed Matthew off the desk.

"Hey!" he said, just barely keeping himself from falling onto the floor.

"Or yours, either. He's a liar!" I could feel tears on my cheeks. I pushed Matthew again, both hands on his chest. He went backward and cracked his head on the upper bunk of our bed. It took him a second to recover, and then he came at me and pushed me back.

"He's not! He's not!"

Next thing I knew, I was hitting at Matthew as hard as I could. At first he just put up his arms to fend me off, but then he started hitting back, and somehow we ended up on the floor, rolling over each other, grabbing and punching, both of us crying now. And Dad was there, hollering at us, dragging us apart.

He sent Matthew downstairs. I sat on my bed, tasting blood in my mouth.

Dad stood there, his arms folded across his chest, and I wondered what he would do. Matthew and I had never fought like that before. Not one time in all our lives.

"It isn't your brother you're mad at, you know." I didn't say anything. "God can handle your anger."

"I don't want him to. I don't want anything more to do with God. I hate him!"

I half expected Dad to hit me, though that was something else that had never happened before. What he did was worse. He nodded. "I know."

I smashed my fist into the wall. He moved toward me and I ducked, but all he did was take my fist in one hand and pull me up from the bed. "Jacob wrestled with an angel," he said, "but they haven't been coming around to serve as sparring partners for us lately. We have to work it out some other way." He dropped my hand. "I suggest you go for a walk. It's not too late."

I don't remember going downstairs. Or opening the door to go out. Suddenly there I was outside, the chilly air coming into my lungs every time I breathed in. I walked, feeling as if every muscle in my body was about to explode, wanting to kick trees, punch out the stars that were just coming out in the darkening sky. And then I was at the Hendricks' house, pounding on the front door.

Dr. Hendricks opened it, a wineglass in his hand, a little out of breath, as if he had run to see what crazy person was banging away like that. Lydia barreled through the door, nearly knocking him down as she came, and bounced around my legs. "I'm sorry,"

I said. "I was out walking, and I thought Lydia might like to come with me."

I heard Colin coughing in the background, over the sound of an opera singer warbling something incomprehensible.

"Certainly," Dr. Hendricks said, and waved me in with his glass. "Colin is—"

"I'll just get her leash and go," I said. "I don't want to bother him."

With Lydia on her leash, I started toward the park, and then, at the corner, I turned instead and started around the block. I didn't want to take her near the lake when I wasn't going to let her dive. I wondered if she'd even want to in the dark, but I didn't feel like finding out. We walked around the block twice, and then we ran around it twice more. Only when Lydia's tongue was hanging out did I slow down again. I didn't want to wear her out. Only myself. If I could have, I'd have run all the way around Bradyville. Anything to make me too tired to want to hit anyone, anything to keep from going home.

When we went back to the house, I sat on the porch steps and Lydia sat with me. I patted her head and rubbed behind her ears. "You don't know what's coming, do you, girl?" I asked her. "That's easier, maybe. Maybe it'll be hard, when he's just gone and you don't know why. But it'll be hard for all of us." I felt the tears start again, and I rubbed them away. I would not cry any more tonight!

When I took her inside, I put away her leash and then went into the living room, where Colin was already in bed, in his pajamas. The bed's head and knee positions were raised the way those television ads show how people can keep their backs from hurting. He was coughing again and he had the oxygen tube in. A box of Kleenex lay on top of the patchwork quilt, against his bony leg. "Sorry," he said when he stopped coughing. "I'm not much company tonight. Hope you had a good walk."

"We did," I said. It wasn't true, but I'd gotten used to letting people think what wasn't true. Anyway, it might have been true for Lydia. "Can't stay. I've got homework." As if I intended to do any homework.

Colin nodded. And began to cough again. He held a Kleenex to his mouth.

"Good night," I said. I turned to Dr. Hendrick, who was sitting in his chair between the stereo speakers. The empty wineglass was on the table next to him and the opera was turned low now. "Good night."

He pushed himself up from the chair and walked with me to the front door, as if he had to show me where it was. When we got there, he glanced over his shoulder. "He has pneumonia," he said, his voice so low I could hardly hear it. "I'm afraid it won't be long now."

As the words sank in, I remembered what I had seen a moment before. Seen and not taken in. The

Kleenex in Colin's hand, blotched with red. If he were a plant, it would have been green.

The porch light was on, and in spite of the chill, a couple of moths flew slowly around it, bumbling into the glass.

I was standing on a high ledge. Down below was a river, a long way down. I needed to get down to it. It was important. The most important thing in the whole world. I knew that the best way to get to the river was to jump, and I kept trying, but I couldn't. Something was holding me back. I turned to see what it was, and there was Matthew, standing above me on top of a cliff. There was a heavy line between us, like a mountain-climbing rope. One end was tied around my waist and the other end was tied around his. He was holding on to it with both hands, leaning back, pulling at it so that it felt as if it was cutting off my air.

"Let go!" I yelled up at him. "You've got to let go. I need to jump!"

He didn't answer. He just kept pulling on the rope, and it kept getting tighter and tighter around my waist. Suddenly I saw that there was a knife in my hand—a huge hunting knife with a sharp edge that gleamed in the sun. Frantically, I started sawing at the rope around my waist, cutting through the strands one after another. As each strand broke, I could feel the pressure easing around my waist, my breath coming more easily. Finally, with a last slash, I cut the final strand. I was free.

"No!" Matthew screamed as I turned back toward the river. "No, no, noooooo!"

I jumped, and saw too late that the rope I'd cut wasn't the only one. There was another, a darker, thinner line that wasn't wrapped around my waist. It went directly into me, straight through the wall of my chest. As I began to fall, I felt a wrench in the center of me. I heard a scraping sound above. I twisted around and saw Matthew, his face contorted with pain, his hands clenched against his chest where the other end of the line disappeared through his shirt. He was being dragged toward the edge of the cliff. And then he went over the edge and both of us were falling toward the river. Except that when I looked, the river had disappeared and we were falling toward a pile of jagged rocks.

I woke up and found myself in bed, the room just beginning to go gray with dawn. My pillow was damp with sweat; my pajama top bunched where both hands clutched it against my chest. Above me, Matthew's mattress bulged downward with his weight. I could hear his breathing, slow and even. It hadn't been one of our twin dreams, then.

CHAPTER TWENTY-TWO

Nobody was up yet. I pulled on a shirt and a pair of pants, jammed my feet into my shoes, and went downstairs. I got out a box of cereal, poured myself a bowl, dumped milk in, and ate, standing at the window over the sink. Sometime in the last week the last of the leaves had changed color on the trees between the house and the church. Red and orange they were, and a dull brown. The wind that was blowing fat gray clouds across the sky was pulling leaves off, too, and scattering them across the grass. When I finished my cereal, I got my backpack from the floor by the back door, where I'd thrown it after school yesterday.

Johnna came out of her room wearing her flannel pajamas. Winter pajamas, I thought. She rubbed her eyes. "It's awful early," she said. "Why are you up?"

"Couldn't sleep," I said. "Go on back to bed. You can sleep another hour."

She cocked her head at me, for all the world like

Lydia, and frowned. "You okay?" she said.

"Sure, I'm okay."

"Your lip's all bruised."

"You should see the other guy." I sighed. "You will see him. Me and Matthew had a fight."

Her eyes got huge. "What about?"

"Never mind," I said. "It's not important. Go back to bed."

"'Matthew and I,' not 'me and Matthew,'" she said. "You're sure you're okay?"

"I told you, I'm fine." I could see she didn't believe me. Maybe it wasn't only twins who knew things other people didn't say. But I couldn't have explained it in a million years. Wouldn't have tried. "Go on now—go back to bed." She stood for a while, and then finally shrugged and went.

I put on my jacket, grabbed a knitted hat out of the closet, and went outside. The wind was blowing hard and cold. It smelled like winter. I was glad of the hat and wished I had gone looking for gloves. Wished I had taken time in the room to put on socks.

Now that I was out, I didn't know what to do. I just couldn't stay in the house, waiting for the rest of the family to wake up. I couldn't sit at the breakfast table, listen to grace, listen to Dad praying for Colin. I couldn't say "Amen" with the rest of them. I couldn't look at Matthew and think about what I was doing—couldn't help doing—to the two of us. I didn't know how I was going to go on at all, being Mark Thomas Filkins, the second in the line of my generation's preachers. Or how I could live in my family as anybody else.

If I were Colin Hendrick's son, I thought, I would be losing my father. But not everything else that has ever mattered in my life.

I walked up one street and down another, keeping my eyes on the sidewalk, scuffing leaves out of the way, trying not to look at their colors, at the chewed edges and the moldy patches. Finally, even though I'd walked at least once around every block between home and there, I got to school. I checked my watch. Still an hour and a half before school started. I sat down under a tree in the corner of the school grounds and leaned back against my backpack. I was freezing. If I had any money, I thought, I could go wait in the coffee shop on Larch Street, have a cup of cocoa. But they didn't let kids hang around inside unless they were buying something. And I didn't have so much as a quarter with me. I shoved my hands deep into my pockets and closed my eyes.

After a while, when my ankles had gone numb, I heard a car engine. Mr. Gladwell, the custodian, had arrived. He pulled his car into his parking place, locked it, and hurried to the side door, his jacket collar pulled up against the wind and his dark gray hair blowing into his eyes. He hadn't noticed me there, under the tree. He unlocked the door and hurried inside, and I watched the door close, wishing I could go in with him, out of the wind. And then I saw that

I could. The door hadn't latched. He hadn't taken the time to wait and pull it shut.

I stayed there a minute, to be sure he'd gone to his office and wouldn't see me, and then I got up and slipped in through the door. It was blessedly warm inside. The light was on in his office, spilling across the hallway. So I went the other way, slipped up the half flight of stairs to the main floor, and went to the science classroom. Mrs. Gerston wouldn't be there for an hour yet. She had her own kids to get off to school in the morning, so she didn't get there till a few minutes before we did.

I wondered if Mrs. Gerston knew that Colin had pneumonia now. Probably. Dr. Hendrick had probably called her. Or maybe she'd been over at their house yesterday, taking another pint of ice cream.

I put my backpack on my desk and then wandered around the classroom. It was dim and shadowy, almost dark, with only the light coming from the windows and the clouds outside seeming to get lower and darker every minute. On the wall were the two big diagrams I had made—the web of life on green poster board, the food chain on red. A few of the open spaces were filled now with reports. Todd's group had finished theirs first, of course, Todd pushing everybody else. But everybody had been working hard. Mrs. Gerston said she'd never seen a class put so much effort into something that wasn't even going to be graded. Somehow Colin had done what he wanted to do. Somehow he'd made everybody care.

It won't be long now, Dr. Hendrick had said. Colin wouldn't come back to teach the class again. We wouldn't take the other field trip he had planned. He wouldn't see the rest of the reports. And he wouldn't be there to tell me what to tell the others about their work. The unit would have to end. I wouldn't be able to take his place again. An apprentice has to have a master. It doesn't work any other way.

I went to the windowsill and stood for a while looking at the mason jar, at the salad bowl full of animalcules. The pond dragon was against the side, its breathing tube in the air at the surface, its jaws open, waiting for something to swim close enough. Even in the dim light, I could see the tiny specks moving jerkily up and down in the greenish brown water. The fine hairs of the algae, clustered at the bottom, looked still and dead. But the green meant they were alive, their chloroplasts like little factories turning light into sugar, however they did it. "Just another mystery we haven't figured out yet," Colin had said. He wouldn't be around to figure it out.

In the aquarium the crayfish moved slowly across one of the rocks. A minnow, staying out of its way, scooted behind a clump of weed. Life was going on here. Going on. Like a clock that just has to be wound up once and then goes along, ticking away forever after, its hands marking out the time even if nobody is there to see—or care.

I picked up the mason jar, feeling the weight of it

in my hand, watching the little specks moving in it, thinking of all the littler specks, the ones I couldn't see without the microscope, moving and moving. And I threw it as hard as I could at the aquarium, where the crayfish had just gone under the rock bridge. The jar shattered the side of the aquarium and water gushed out like a tidal wave across the shelf, splashing onto the floor, splashing my bare ankles. Water and glass went everywhere. Minnows flopped onto the shelf and then down onto the floor. The crayfish had gone with the first rush of water and was scrabbling feebly among bits of glass under a desk. The mason jar, unhurt, lay on its side in the broken aquarium, emptying the last of its water and algae and moving specks—all the little live things—over the side and onto the floor. I swept the salad bowl off the windowsill. It hit the radiator valve as it fell and shattered, spitting glass and water at my legs.

I crossed the room then, crunching glass, slipping on the wet floor, and tore the posters down off the wall. I ripped them into pieces so small that no two of my Magic Marker letters could be read together. I let the pieces fall on the floor like the leaves off the trees. The colors of life. Green like chlorophyll. Red like blood. I was still doing that when Mr. Gladwell arrived and dragged me away.

CHAPTER TWENTY-THREE

Mr. Gladwell, holding on to the back of my jacket and pushing me ahead of him, took me to the office, even though Dr. Barth, the principal, wasn't there yet. Even though there were only two of us in the whole building. I thought at first he might call the police. But he just sat me down on the bench by the secretary's desk. The whole time he didn't talk to me, as if I were an animal of some kind and couldn't have understood him. He just kept shaking his head and muttering "Vandalism" and "What's the world coming to?" under his breath. "Stay right there!" he said to me finally. Like saying "Sit, stay!" to a dog. I sat. I stayed. He went out, without turning on the light, closing the door and leaving me in the dim light from the one window, whose shade was halfway down.

I looked down at my hands, closed into fists on my knees. I opened them. Shreds of green fluttered to the floor.

Time must have passed, because time does, but I couldn't feel it, couldn't feel anything. Images kept replaying themselves in my mind—the gush of water carrying the crayfish, its antennae waving, through the shattered wall of that little world we'd created for him. He'd been safe in there. Safer than he would have been in the creek, out with the raccoons and the herons and the pollution. In the aquarium he had been the top of the food chain. Had he known that? Had he thought he was safe, living in that glass box, with us to feed him? Well, he wasn't safe. His building blocks could get rearranged, too. Anytime.

It occurred to me that I'd finally succeeded in driving the prayer out of my head. My brain wasn't repeating it anymore. It had traded words without meaning for images without meaning. Water gushing. Glass shattering.

Glass shattering. I looked down at my ankles. Blood loses its redness when it dries. There were dots and lines and little drips of dark brown where the glass bits had broken the skin. I couldn't feel that, either.

Finally, Miss Weinstein, the school secretary, came in and turned the lights on. She jumped when she saw me, as if she'd encountered a snake. "What are you doing here . . . ?" she asked, leaving the place where the name was supposed to be blank. Matthew or Mark? she must have been thinking. Who is this?

But right behind her came Dr. Barth and Mr.

Gladwell, the custodian talking about vandalism, broken glass, dead fish, mess. "The computers?" Dr. Barth asked, and Mr. Gladwell shook his head. "Well, that's a blessing!"

Dr. Barth looked at me. "What have you to say for yourself . . . ?" And he, too, left the name place blank.

"Mark," I said. Because that was the only thing I had to say for myself.

Dr. Barth said something to Miss Weinstein about calling my parents, but before she could do that, other people came in, a substitute asking for lesson plans, teachers checking their mailboxes on the wall next to the door. Some of them noticed me, started to say something, and then became busy with something else, and I realized that my ID bracelet was caught up inside my jacket sleeve. I could have said I was Matthew and Dr. Barth, Miss Weinstein, and certainly Mr. Gladwell would have believed me. "Mark," I said quietly. "Mark Thomas Filkins."

"What?" Miss Weinstein said. "Did you say something?"

I just shook my head.

When Mrs. Gerston came, she glanced my way. "Mark?" was all she said. She hadn't needed the ID bracelet. Then she went into Dr. Barth's office and closed the door behind her. After a while she came out, and I saw that her eyes looked a little puffy. "It would be better for you to be at home today," she said. "I'll drive you if you'd like. Dr. Barth will take my classes till I get back."

"Am I suspended?" I asked.

"Officially, yes. What you did—" She seemed to be looking at something on the wall over my head. The only thing there was an antidrug poster. "What you did has to be classed as vandalism. The school can't just let it go. And I can't say that I understand it exactly. But I know that it wasn't what it looks like. Let's just say that sending you home serves two purposes here."

"Do you know about . . . ?"

She nodded. "Dr. Hendrick called this morning."

Mrs. Gerston came into the house with me. Dad had gone off to the apartment building he manages, but Mom was there. They talked in the kitchen and I went up to my room, took off my clothes, and crawled into bed in my underwear. Being home on a school day had always meant staying in bed. Mom bringing me Jell-O and hot tea. Sometimes those things made me feel better. This time nothing would.

Mom came up after Mrs. Gerston left. She sat on the edge of my bed the way she does when I'm sick. I almost expected her to feel my forehead for a fever. "Do you know why you did it?" she asked.

I shook my head.

"You know it was wrong. . . ."

"I know."

"Did it help?"

"Nothing helps."

She put her hand on my shoulder and I was just able to keep from shaking it off. "I wish you'd told us about the pneumonia. It must have been a rough night."

I nodded.

"I wish I knew how to help you with this. Some things we just have to get through on our own. But know this, Mark, no matter how it feels to you right now, God is here with you. He doesn't desert us. Not ever."

Now I did shake her hand off. If you jump toward the river, you see it's all rocks, I thought.

"Sleep for a while if you can. I'm working at the church office today. I'll call Dr. Hendrick in a while and ask if you can go over to visit later."

I slept. And this time I didn't dream.

After lunch, I walked to the Hendricks' house. It was still blustery, chilly, gray. This time I had socks and gloves. They didn't help a lot.

It was a nurse who let me in. "He'll be glad you came," she told me. Lydia wasn't there. She must be in the yard, I thought. Dr. Hendrick was in his chair in the living room, a book in his lap, as if he'd forgotten it was there. There was no music playing. He nodded at me, unsmiling. He looked as if he were made out of carved granite. Solid and unmovable.

"Look who's come to see you," the nurse said to Colin, and she sounded as if she might be talking to an eight-year-old, not a Nobel Prize winner. I would have liked to kick her.

I thought Colin had already changed as much as a person can. But I was wrong. Now, in the bed in the living room, he looked like someone else, someone who'd begun to die already. He turned his head to look at me and that something that had always been there behind his eyes, so intense it practically jumped at you, had faded. He smiled, but the smile, too, was missing something. The oxygen tube was in his nose, and I could hear the ragged, almost bubbling sound of his breath. If he'd been hanging on to life with both hands, he was letting go of it now. "Hang on!" I wanted to yell at him. "Don't leave. Not yet!"

I pulled a dining room chair over and sat down close to the bed. "I got suspended," I told him. "First suspension in the history of the Filkins family."

He frowned. "What'd you do?" His voice was raspy and weak.

"Wrecked the food chain," I said. "Tore the web."'

He reached out his hand, and I let him take mine in his. "You okay?"

And then I was crying. No transition, no working up to it. Feeling like a fool, I put my head down on the quilt, holding on to his hand as if it would stop me falling. He pushed himself up and leaned toward me so that he could reach me with the other hand

and patted me the way people pat crying babies.

"It's all right," he said.

"No!" I said when I could talk. "It isn't all right. Nothing will ever be all right again."

"Mark!" he said. I looked up, and the light was there in his eyes again. Colin was back, hanging on. "It's the way things work. So it *is* all right."

He sank back into his pillows. If he'd meant to say anything else, he didn't have the energy. Or the breath.

"Aren't you scared?" I asked.

"Well, *sure.*" He waited a minute to get his breath. "You think I'm stupid?"

I wiped my eyes and did my best to smile. "Are you kidding? A Nobel laureate stupid?" I thought about what he'd said about heaven and hell. That there was no room for either of them in the universe we know. But we don't know anything. He'd said that, too. "I wish you would let me know if it's okay," I said. "After. I wish you could."

He squeezed my hand. But he was fading again, and I couldn't be sure if he'd even heard me. It was dumb anyway. How could building blocks let me know anything? He'd closed his eyes now, and his breathing, that awful bubbling sound, seemed to fill the room. I knew it was a sound I would never forget for the rest of my life.

I spent the rest of the afternoon in the park with Lydia. It seemed to me too cold for diving, but she insisted, so I threw her rock for her for a while. This time, when she shook herself, flinging water on my jeans, I thought of all the little live things in the pond, all the little live things that would be in those drops. Being shaken out into the cold, dry world. "If it isn't one thing, it's another," I told them.

When I decided Lydia was done, we jogged around the baseball diamond a couple of times to get her warmed up again. This time I didn't envy her, living her life as if nothing was happening back home. Maybe Colin had already said the last thing he would ever say to her, and she didn't know it. Would never remember it.

When we got back to the house, the nurse was gone and Colin was asleep, the sound of his breathing still filling the living room. Dr. Hendrick was in the kitchen, fixing himself a bowl of soup for dinner. He wasn't making anything for Colin. He thanked me for walking Lydia.

"Anytime," I told him. "I mean that. Anytime. Always."

He reached down and patted her on the head. He knew what I was saying. "Thank you. She'll like that."

I stood by Colin's bed awhile, watching his chest rise and fall as he slept. Watching life be life for as long as it could.

"I'll be back tomorrow," I whispered. When I left it was beginning to spit rain.

CHAPTER TWENTY-FOUR

When I got home, I stood outside for a while, getting up the nerve to go in. I can't do this, I thought. It's too hard. But there was nothing else to do, nowhere else to go. Dad was in the dining room, working on his sermon for Sunday, and the others were in the kitchen, getting supper ready. Mom was pouring hot spaghetti into the colander in the sink, steam rising around her and fogging up her glasses.

Luke was pouring the milk. "You're late," he said. "You're supposed to be setting the table."

"It's done already," Matthew said.

Johnna was folding napkins. "You said you were fine this morning," she said accusingly. "But then you went and got *suspended*!" Maybe Johnna will be a policewoman, I thought, instead of a preacher. "Daddy wants to see you. You're in trouble." Mom shushed her.

In trouble. Johnna didn't begin to know how right she was.

Dad wasn't as angry as I'd expected him to be. He said I'd be responsible for getting a new aquarium for the classroom, and replacing Dr. Hendrick's salad bowl. He didn't mention salvaging the ruined science project. Nobody could do that. Then he told me that we couldn't keep from having feelings, especially in tough times, but even in the toughest times, we could choose how we would express them. He said he hoped I would be able to find better ways from now on. Then he said he hoped it would be a lot of years before I had to handle such a tough time again. Most of the rest of it was just about the same as Mom had said that morning. It seemed like everybody could feel God near me except me.

Mom called in to say that supper was on the table, and Dad rubbed his bald spot and stood up, leaving the legal pad and pen and the balls of crumpled paper on the table. "You want to know what I'm preaching about Sunday?"

I shrugged.

"John fourteen:twenty-seven. 'Not as the world giveth give I unto you.' *Not as the world giveth,* Mark. Most of us miss that part of the message."

All through dinner I felt Matthew next to me, as if there was static electricity building up between us. It felt like if I leaned closer to him, blue lightning would snap between us. I did my best to ignore it. I concentrated on wrapping noodles around my fork, getting each bite to my mouth without spattering my shirt with sauce.

Because I was suspended, I didn't have any homework to do. So I stayed in the living room and watched television instead. It kept me away from Matthew, who had gone upstairs. I thought of him up there at the desk, doing his work as if there was nothing different happening in the world. Or maybe not like that. Maybe as if just doing the regular stuff could take care of what was happening, make it regular, too. But if that's what he thought, he was wrong. I sat through program after program, but I couldn't have said afterward what any of them had been about. What's happening at Colin's? I kept wondering. Was he breathing? Was he coughing his blood out into a Kleenex? Did he have enough medication to keep him from hurting? If I were his son, I'd be able to be there at least.

At eleven Mom made me turn off the television and go up to bed. Luke was already asleep. Matthew was in bed, but I knew the minute I walked in that he wasn't asleep yet.

"Are you all right?" he whispered. He didn't have to whisper to keep from waking Luke up. Luke could sleep through bombs going off.

"No, I'm not all right!" I said.

"Okay. I know that."

"Just do me a favor, will you? Don't tell me God's with me. Because he isn't! Maybe he's with you, but he's not with me."

Matthew sat up in bed. "He isn't with me, either. If he was, I'd know what to say."

"Don't say anything."

So he lay back down and we didn't talk any more.

It took me a long time to go to sleep. As I lay there, listening to Matthew toss and turn and sigh above me, I thought of the prayer we had said before bed when we were little. Probably the first prayer I ever learned. "Now I lay me down to sleep, I pray the Lord my soul to keep. If I should die before I wake, I pray the Lord my soul to take." Why do people teach children that prayer? I wondered. And why had it never scared me?

I must have gone to sleep eventually, because I woke up with a jerk. The light was on, bright and golden, making me blink. I was facing the wall. I turned over. And my heart seemed to stop. Standing next to the bed, dressed in jeans and a plaid shirt, was Colin Hendrick. I blinked. "Mark," he said, his voice urgent. And I realized what had wakened me. It had been Colin saying my name.

"Colin? Is that really you?"

He didn't answer my question. He just stood there, looking at me, frowning slightly. Of course it was him. I could see that for myself.

Then he smiled and held his arms out.

"What?" I asked.

"Here I am—scientific proof. I just wanted you to know that. You were right!"

I sat up. "Right about what?"

"Think about it. *You know.*" He smiled again, and then he was gone and it was dark in the room. One moment he was there and the next he wasn't. I pushed back the covers and got out of bed, the floor cold under my bare feet. The only light was from the alarm, glowing greenly on the dresser. It was 3:34.

I had seen Colin standing there next to the bed. He'd talked to me. The light had been on. Now it was off. The door was closed. And then I understood. Of course it was closed. It had been a dream. Nobody had come in and nobody had gone out. I'd had a dream and now I was awake, my bare feet on the cold floor.

I got back into bed. I lay there, shivering under my blanket, trying to get warm again, going over the dream so I'd remember it in the morning. Colin, dressed the way he always used to dress. Looking the way he always used to look, not that shrunken figure in the hospital bed. *You were right!* About what?

I began to feel warm then. As warm as if I were wrapped in a down comforter. Dream or not, it had been wonderful to see him there looking like his old self. Better than his old self. I thought of the first time I'd seen him in the park. Just some stranger with a miracle diving dog. Some stranger in baggy clothes—

Suddenly, it occurred to me that Colin Hendrick was already sick when I met him. If he hadn't been, he wouldn't have come home to Bradyville. Wouldn't have been in the park with Lydia. If Colin Hendrick hadn't been dying, I never would have met him in the first place.

It was early when I woke up again. Not yet six o'clock. I sat up and threw my feet over the edge of the bed. There was something I needed to remember. A dream—

"What were you right about?"

I jumped at the sound of Matthew's groggy voice. "What?"

"Colin Hendrick told you you were right. About what?"

And the dream was back as if it had just happened. Every detail clear. I stood up and grabbed Matthew by the shoulders. "That was my dream. Did you have it, too?"

"I guess so."

"What happened?"

Matthew rubbed his eyes and sat up. "Colin Hendrick was in the room, standing by the bed—and it was very bright, so bright I couldn't see at first—and he called your name. Then he said he was scientific proof and you were right."

"And I asked him about what—"

"And he said to think about it. He said you know."

"Only I don't," I said.

"Then he was gone, and you got out of bed. In the dark."

"That's when I woke up."

Matthew nodded. "Me too, I guess. I checked the clock."

"Three-thirty-four," I said.

"Yeah. So what do you think the dream means?"

I shrugged. "I don't know. It was just a dream."

Luke was asleep, but I knew I couldn't sleep again. Neither could Matthew. We got up and dressed and went downstairs. Matthew put on the teakettle and we made cocoa. "I think it's a good thing we're dreaming together again," he said when we were sitting at the table, poking at the marshmallows in our mugs with spoons. We both liked to hold them under till they melted.

"I don't think it means what you think it does," I said.

"We'll always be twins," he said, and I knew we both knew what we were saying, even if we hadn't put it all into words.

I nodded. And sipped at my cocoa. It burned my tongue.

"Ouch," he said, and we both laughed.

"Was that for real?" I asked.

"No."

"It won't be the same anymore," I told him. "Not ever."

I thought he might argue with me, but he didn't. He just nodded as he stirred his cocoa. "We've had different lives now," he said.

I hadn't thought of it that way. What had he been

doing all this time when I had been with Colin? I didn't know. Of course I didn't. How could I have thought that *I* was the only one whose life had angled off, like a path changing direction in the woods? Our paths had split, mine going one way, his another. One Mark and one Matthew.

The phone rang then, jangling so that we both jumped, and my cocoa spilled, burning my hand almost as badly as it had burned my tongue. I hurried out into the hall to pick it up before it could ring again. As I lifted the receiver I understood what it means to say your heart is in your throat. I could hardly breathe. Could hardly make my mouth say, "Filkins residence, Mark speaking."

"Mark." That was all Dr. Hendrick needed to say. All he did say for a minute, as I heard him swallowing and swallowing again. "I hope I'm not calling too early."

"No."

"I wanted to tell you that Colin died during the night. I was with him. He went peacefully."

Peacefully! What could he have done, so thin and weak in the bed, to go any other way? "When?" I managed.

And even as he said it, I knew. "Around three-thirty."

"Three-thirty-four," I said.

There was a silence at the other end of the line. Then: "Yes. That would be about right."

"Are you all right?" I asked, as Matthew had

asked me last night. What a stupid question it was. I knew the answer.

"Ginny Gerston is here," he said. "I'm managing."

"I'm sorry," I said. It seemed another stupid thing to say. What could anyone say that wasn't stupid?

"Yes. Well. I have other calls to make."

"Thank you for telling me."

I didn't cry. I set the phone down and stood looking at it for a minute. Then I turned. Matthew was standing in the kitchen doorway. Mom and Dad were at the top of the stairs, Mom with her hand pressed to her mouth, Dad with one arm around her. "Colin died," I said, hearing my voice as if it came from a long way away. "At three-thirty-four."

Matthew looked at me. "That was when . . ."

I nodded. I understood now. "Colin came and woke us up."

CHAPTER TWENTY-FIVE

Bradyville was famous on the day of Colin's funeral. People came from all over the country, scientists who had worked with him, people who had known him in college and graduate school. Executives from the oil companies that had funded his research. Television networks with cameras and vans with satellite dishes on their roofs. Even the governor of Ohio. My family was there, about halfway back in St. John's Episcopal, but Dr. Hendrick had me sit up in the first pew with Mrs. Gerston and him. I couldn't look at the coffin, gleaming with a big spray of flowers on top. It didn't seem to have anything to do with Colin, even though I knew that his body had to be inside. A lot of people told stories about him and read poems.

Dr. Hendrick had asked me to say something, and at first I said no. I was afraid I might cry if I tried. But I thought a lot about it and decided I needed to do it. I wrote it out and practiced it over and over, getting all my tears used up, saying it to Matthew until he knew it better than I did.

When it was my turn, I went up to the front of the church—the church Colin had gone to when he was a little boy. I looked out at all the people, maybe ten times as many as could fit in Dad's church even if we set up extra chairs. "Colin Hendrick made me his apprentice," I said. "Sometimes that meant I took his dog, Lydia, to the park." People laughed at that. "But mostly it meant he taught me about science. He taught me about the web of life and how everyone and everything is connected. He taught me that we know so much science now that no one person, no matter how smart, can fit it all into his head. And he also taught me that we don't know anything yet. That the universe is so complex that most of it is still a mystery. It was a mystery he loved and spent his whole life exploring. He didn't have as much time as he wanted.

"He used to tell me that when we die, we get recycled. We go back to being the building blocks of life, and those building blocks will be used again. Well, I think he was right about that. You don't get a Nobel Prize for being stupid." People laughed again. "Our bodies do get recycled. But bodies aren't all we are. I used to tell him I believed that, but now I *know* it. It was the very last thing he taught me.

"There's a whole lot I don't understand. But I'm just about the luckiest eighth grader in the world to have had such a teacher, even for a little while. And for as long as he needs me to, I'll keep taking Lydia to the park."

Were Matthew and I dreaming that night? I don't think so, and neither does he. I *do* know what Colin meant when he told me I was right. It was about soul. What he hadn't believed in before because there was no way to prove it. Not everybody would believe the proof he found that night, but it was all *he* needed, and he was a noble lariat. So it's plenty of proof for me.

Colin didn't change his mind before he died and become a Christian. But the light in our room that night wasn't about something bad happening to him because of it. I don't have any doubt about that at all. Or about Colin's smile. I'd asked him to let me know, if he could, if death was okay, and he had. I asked Dad about the rest of it. About having to take Jesus for your personal Savior, and "I am the way, and the truth, and the life."

What Dad said was, "We don't know all the answers." He meant it differently from Colin, but I think he was saying the same thing. "God's bigger than we are. 'My thoughts are not your thoughts, neither are my ways your ways, saith the Lord.' I suppose it could be that Jesus didn't mean we have to accept him *before* we die. If he came to us on our way out, as it were, why couldn't we make the choice then?"

"Like Thomas the doubter," I said. "When we can

really *see* him." I liked that. I don't know if Dad was right, but I don't need to. I think that's one of the mysteries we don't know enough to understand.

It's hard to go to Dr. Hendrick's house knowing that Colin isn't there and that he'll never be there again, but I go every day to get Lydia and take her to the park. As sad as both of us are (and I can tell she's sad, even if she is a dog), it helps a lot that we still have each other. She still likes diving for her rock, just like I still like playing soccer—I went back to the team after the funeral—but neither of us has as much fun doing those things as we used to.

Matthew goes to the park with us a lot of the time now. Lydia doesn't ever get the two of us confused. Not even for a second. He doesn't understand why sometimes when she brings the rock back and shakes all over us, I have to blink back tears all of a sudden. I don't blame him—I don't understand either why it just hits me like that sometimes. Dad says grief is like a broken leg. It hurts like crazy and it takes a long, long time to heal. But eventually it does, he says. Eventually you can walk again.

The web of life doesn't work without death. Carolyn Dirkman was right that day Matthew and I preached our first sermon—the day I met Colin. If we could get what we *want* just by asking God for it, nobody would ever die. We're too scared of it. And losing people hurts too much. The sermons we gave that day were too simple. Like Colin always said, the universe is about complexity. Next time I give a sermon, I'll try to remember that.

There's one Mark and one Matthew now—two different people. But on the soccer field we can still pass the ball back and forth the way we did before. The twin thing—one of Colin's ordinary miracles.

STEPHANIE S. TOLAN

has explored compelling social issues in many superb novels for young adults, including *A Good Courage* and *Plague Year.* She is also well-known for writing such shivery ghost stories as *Who's There?* and *The Face in the Mirror.* Of *Welcome to the Ark,* the first in a planned trilogy, ALA *Booklist* noted that "Tolan blends elements of science fiction with nonstop suspense in a provocative, disturbingly real story."

Save Halloween!, the first book about the fundamentalist Filkins family, tells what happens when Johnna, Matthew and Mark's younger sister, decides to help write her school's Halloween pageant against her father's wishes. *Kirkus Reviews* praised the book's "several nicely realized characters of quiet courage, refreshingly committed to their faith," and it was chosen as a *Booklist* Children's Editors' Choice.

Stephanie S. Tolan lives in Charlotte, North Carolina.